G.O.R.E SECTOR
BOOK 2

HALF-MOON TRENCH

A NOVEL BY MICHAEL COLE

SEVEREDPRESS

HALF-MOON TRENCH

ISBN: 978-1-923165-82-3

CHAPTER 1

Scarlett Caldera.
Half-Moon Trench, Pacific Ocean – Three miles deep.

"Hurry! The escape pods are up this way!"

Running feet drummed against the steel flooring. Corridor B-Charlie had turned dark, save for a few emergency lights that had already dimmed.

Had it not been for the security officer, Mel Haysen would be running in circles—more likely, he would have joined the rest of his ill-fated crew. As the geologist for the deep-sea station *Scarlett Caldera*, he was always focused on his work and not much else. He knew the way to the lab, Operations, Airlock Station Alpha and Bravo, the galley, and his own quarters. Not much else.

A horrible rumbling echoed through the *Scarlett Caldera*. It had been hit hard. Though he could not see through the thick steel walls, he could envision the black ocean outside and the demonic presence lurking within it. For all he knew, the beast had been down here for thousands of years. Millions, maybe. Only to be disturbed by the hubris of mankind. Specifically, the corporate juggernaut that was the Brom-Caylen Corporation.

Dominant in a multitude of markets including food production, real estate, pharmaceuticals, and even entertainment, Brom-Caylen had quickly risen into being a mega-company in less than a decade. Its influence could be felt everywhere, including the military and federal government. Now, they were branching into the next market, one that would elevate its founder to an untouchable status.

Renewable energy.

Down here in the Half-Moon Trench, the scientists employed by Brom-Caylen believed to have found the answer. Six months ago, Mel Haysen had been given the opportunity of a lifetime. Up until now, he had been working in geological surveying for various institutes and companies, eventually obtaining a position surveying undersea territory for undersea naval stations. Underwater construction was another industry the company dominated. Two years ago, Mel was the geologist for a construction job a few miles off the coast of Costa Rica, contracted by the U.S. Navy to build an underwater submarine base. It was a large project with significant pay—enough for Mel to resort to devious means to beat out an old colleague who was a runner-up for the position.

Following the completion of the project, he was asked by one of the vice presidents for his input regarding a project in the Half-Moon Trench. Lo and behold, the *Scarlett Caldera* was constructed and the deep-sea mining project had commenced.

Before long, the operation was hauling three tons of trench core rock per day. With his one-and-a-half share, Mel was watching his bank account and his career skyrocket in a short time. With no personal life topside, he was content with staying in the *Scarlett Caldera* for the foreseeable future. Why not? With the money he was earning, he wanted to be nowhere else but here.

Today, he wanted to be anywhere else but here. To hell with the money. What good was it if he was dead?

As he ran through the long corridor, he tried to make sense of what had happened. For two years, the station remained undisturbed, until today. There was no denying the reality of their situation. The mining crew outside must have dug too deep.

As a result, they angered something. Many somethings.

Fluorescent lights flickered—the ones that remained functional, at least. The dull beige paintjob in the

2

corridors was usually on full display during the daytime hours. At 2100, most of the lights switched off to simulate night. At the moment, it was not quite so dark as that, but regardless, it was enough to add to Mel's sense of anxiety. For all he knew, all the lights could switch off any minute. All it would take was another hit from the big one.

"Hold up!" The guard came to a sudden stop, throwing his hands out to keep Mel from going any further. Mel froze and listened. He wasn't sure what the guard was hearing.

The man turned to put his ear to the bulkhead. As he did, Mel caught a glimpse of his nametag. Nathan Tay. He had seen the guy a hundred times by now, maybe exchanged a couple of halfhearted hellos. Mel didn't think much of the security guys. He was too preoccupied with his own duties to be bothered learning any of their names. As far as he knew, all they were here to do was keep the staff in check in the event they went stir crazy, and maybe perform routine checks on the equipment and gauges. In the two years he had been down here, not a single issue arose. At least, not one pertaining to disorderly staff.

Nathan Tay put his ear to the bulkhead. His eyes widened. "Whoa. Something's going on out there."

"Yeah, no shit, Sherlock," Mel replied. "I thought we were on our way out of here. Come on, let's get to the damn life pods."

Nathan kept his ear to the steel wall. "I'm not sure if that'll be a good idea."

"Pardon me?"

The guard waved Mel over. Groaning, the geologist stepped to the bulkhead and listened to whatever was going on outside.

Now he could hear it. He felt he was listening to a howling storm. The water outside this part of the station seemed to be in a fit of rage. There was no doubt he was listening to an intense water current.

"Oh, great," Mel muttered. "What's causing that? Don't tell me another vent ruptured."

"Don't think so," Nathan said.

Mel snorted. What would this guy know about that?

"Listen!" Nathan continued. He waited a few moments and, "Right there! That was an impact sound. Something struck something else."

"Hmm…" Mel nodded. Maybe the guard was smarter than the stereotype he had pegged him for. He heard the sound again. It was definitely an impact of some sort, but not against the station. "Has to be the big one."

"What's it doing?" Nathan asked. "It's not attacking us."

"Maybe it found one of the diggers and thought it was a threat," Mel suggested. "Don't really care. Right now, I just want to get to the damn life pods." He moved away from the bulkhead and held his arms out impatiently. "Now, can we please?"

The guard resumed leading him down the escape route.

"There's that juncture up ahead. We'll turn left and that'll take us to the starboard dock… wait!"

For a second time, he came to a sudden stop. He threw his arms out, halting Mel.

"For the love of God!"

"Shh!"

Both men listened. This sound was not one of rushing water or thumping impacts outside the station. This was coming from within the intersecting passageway. Repeated thumps. Running footsteps.

Nathan aimed a flashlight into the juncture right as two individuals emerged. Mel recognized the taller one with balding hair straight away. It was John Fleece, the Second Team foreman.

"Oh, geez!" he said, visibly pleased to recognize the guard's face. There was hardly any acknowledgement for Mel. John approached alongside a slightly shorter man with a four-day beard and thinning hair. His nametag read Daniel Letterman.

"Thought we were the only ones left," Nathan said.

"Almost," Daniel replied.

Nathan and Mel joined the two men in the juncture and took a glance down the corridor.

"Nobody else made it?" Nathan asked.

John shook his head. "No. Most of the guys were near Airlock Station Alpha when... when those things..." He took a deep breath through gritted teeth, then pointed down Corridor B-February. "You don't want to go that way. Trust me."

"*They're* already over there?" Mel asked. John nodded. "You sure?"

John sneered. "Why don't you ask Pete and Takashi."

"What's left of them," Daniel said.

"Christ!" Mel turned around and began to pace in the dwindling glow of flickering fluorescent lights. With each passing moment, the inside of *Scarlett Caldera* was beginning to look like a giant tomb. He was more than happy to make money here, but there was no way in hell he was going to die here. "I'm not dying in this place."

Nathan, who had been calm and collected up to this point, was getting increasingly jittery. "I, uh... I don't know what to do. The life pods were that way."

"We just came from there," Daniel said. "The place is infested."

"I can't stay here," Mel said, barely withholding a mad yell. "Are there any other escape pods?"

Nathan turned to the right, looking northward up Corridor B-Charlie. "There's a stairwell at the end here. Should take us up to A Deck. Might be a couple pods up that way."

Mel was already on the move. "You guys can stay here if you want. I'm checking it out."

The three staff members groaned, then followed the geologist up the corridor. Four pairs of boots reverberated against the steel deck, each pair of eyes frequently glancing down the path whence they came, fearing the sight of those insectoid shapes moving in the dim light.

Mel arrived at the northmost end of the corridor. To his left was a watertight door leading to a stairwell.

"Perfect." He yanked the door open and took a step inside.

"Hold on!" Nathan yelled as he arrived at the door. He had his hand out, his head tilted so his ear was pointed upward. "Just a sec, I think I—"

"Oh, for godsake!" Mel exclaimed. "That damn ear of yours. Can you stop getting freaked out by every little thing you think you hear?!"

"Wait." Nathan tried blocking the way, his eyes fixed on the vents inside the stairwell chamber. "I'm serious. I think there's something—"

THUMP!

All eyes went to the east bulkhead. The strange event taking place outside resulted in a powerful impact against the ocean floor. Judging from the echo and shockwave, Mel estimated it was within a hundred feet of the support legs.

He leaned over Nathan's arm and peeked up into the stairwell. "There's nothing there!"

"Listen, Doctor..."

"No, *you* listen," Mel said. "The big one might breach the hull at any moment. I'd like to be floating topside before then."

"I'm with the doc. Sorry, Nate." With that said, Daniel forced the security officer to the side and made his way up the first set of steps. Mel and John were right behind him, leaving the flabbergasted Nathan at the doorway.

"No, no... WAIT!"

Daniel reached the quarter-space landing and turned to ascend the next set of steps, paying no attention to the scraping sound coming from behind the wall. Not until the vent burst outward, making way for a pair of black arms.

Claws lined with wedge-shaped spurs seized the frightened miner, cutting through clothing and flesh. Squealing, Daniel was yanked from the stair and pulled into the hole in the bulkhead.

The other three men froze, shocked by the unexpected event and torn between helping Daniel or continuing on for their own safety. The sight of warm blood jetting from the open vent and the horrendous gagging sound from the dying worker ended the internal debate.

Mel hurried up the steps, with John on his tail.

With no other option, Nathan raced up the steps, making sure to keep as much distance as possible from the open vent as he passed by it.

The three men arrived on A Deck. The lights were flickering up here too. On the south side, Mel spotted a porthole. He took a moment to glance outside. Most of the exterior lights had been disabled—either from power being disconnected, or smashed entirely.

He could feel another rush of water through the bulkhead. It made him think of his childhood during a severe thunderstorm, when the wind could practically be felt through the walls of his house. Only in that case, there was nothing but weather to fear. Down here, deep in the Half-Moon Trench, there was darkness, crushing pressure, and man-eating predators.

"This way," Nathan said. He made a left turn and took them several yards up the passageway. They came to a set of mechanical steel doors leading to a large chamber. Nathan pulled out his electronic badge, looked at the flickering lights, and shuddered. "Hopefully this'll still work."

He swiped his badge through the scanner. Much to his relief, the doors opened. Inside were the berths for three emergency escape pods, all of which were reserved for the station's leading officers. Two of them had already jettisoned. Fortunately, one remained.

The teepee-shaped escape pod had enough room for three people. Though Mel did not say it out loud, he was grateful Daniel had been caught by the creatures, for it spared them the debate of who would stay behind. He pushed past Nathan and opened the pod door.

"Let's stop wasting time," he said. "Get in."

Nathan approached the door, only to pause after looking at the monitor. "Hold on."

"Don't tell me you hear another funny sound," Mel said.

"No, the airlock is jammed," Nathan replied. "That's why this one wasn't used."

Mel turned around and butted his head against the bulkhead. "You've got to be kidding me!"

"Hang on, I think we can fix it," John said.

"You sure?" Nathan asked.

John went to a ladder on the western side of the chamber. "Yeah. I had to work on this airlock a couple of months ago. There's a lot of residue that accumulates in there. Just give me a second." He climbed a ladder and made his way to a small hatch in the ceiling, just a few yards away from the interior airlock. He disappeared into the ceiling, then quickly reemerged. "Nathan, there's a tool kit near the desk. Should be a big wrench and a can of rust dissolver spray in there."

Nathan sprinted for the workbench on the eastern side of the room. Beside the desk was a small supply closet. In the back was the bag John was talking about. He grabbed the two items and carefully climbed the ladder to the hatch.

Mel took a seat and strapped himself in. All he could do was wait while the workers attempted to rectify their situation. Gazing out through the porthole, he could barely see the overhead hatch where John was working. A series of banging and cursing echoed through the opening, until finally, John poked his head out.

"Okay, try it now."

Nathan went to the control module and pressed the button to open the interior airlock. Red lights flashed and an automated voice sounded off, *"Inner lock open."*

The security guard smiled as the big doors parted. "Thank God. Now, get down here, John, and we'll get the hell out of here!"

John smiled too. Only for a moment. Then he screamed. He reached out and grabbed the top ladder bar with both hands. In that split-second, his body went taut at a perfect forty-five-degree angle. His lower body, still trapped in the hatch, swayed left and right. John reared his head back and hollered.

"Oh, CHRIST! Get them off!"

A stream of blood jetted from the corner of the hatch. Right then, John was suddenly free. His lower body fell clear of the hatch, save for his legs, which had been sliced off at the knees.

Weakened by pain, shock, and blood loss, John lost his grip. He smacked down hard on the deck, blood pumping from his stubs.

"John!" Nathan yelled out. The good-natured security guard raced to the worker's side. "Come on, man. Hang in there. We've got to go!"

Watching through the porthole, Mel watched as a series of insectoid bodies began squeezing through the open hatch. Right below them were Nathan and John. The guard hooked his arms around John's torso and began pulling him toward the escape pod.

Mel's eyes went to the creatures on the ceiling, back to the men, and up again to the ceiling. Nathan and John were just a few steps from the pod door. Yet, the things were descending quickly.

"The hell with this."

He slammed his fist against the large red button near the door, activating the launching process. The pod's door slammed shut and hissed as it went airtight. Seeing this, Nathan dropped John and ran to the porthole, slamming his fist against it while cursing at Mel.

"You bastard! Open the door! Open it!"

The platform lifted, bringing the pod into the airlock. Nathan banged his fist against the hull until he was left stranded on the deck with John. By now, several of the creatures were scurrying down the walls like roaches, each one intent on getting to the fresh meat below. Creatures ranging from four to seven feet in body length, they moved remarkably fast.

Mel, both fascinated and horrified, could not bring himself to look away as they set upon Nathan and John. The latter appeared to be on the verge of unconsciousness, which possibly spared him the agony of being eaten alive. Nathan, on the other hand, attempted to make an escape through the chamber door, only to be pulled to the floor by one of the crustaceans. The guard twisted and turned while multiple creatures dismembered him and slit his abdomen open, revealing an assortment of soft, delicious organs.

The pod was successfully lifted into the airlock. Mechanical arms extended from the walls and held the vehicle in place while the platform sank and the inner lock doors closed. Water soon filled the airlock. Pressure readings flashed inside the pod.

The exterior doors parted and the pod was launched skyward.

Mel exhaled, feeling the release of his tension. He had made it out alive. The memory of those creatures would never leave his consciousness, but at least he survived the nightmare. For now, there was nothing to do except enjoy the ride to safety. With that in mind, he shut his eyes and took in a deep breath.

THUMP!

Mel's eyes opened. The pod rotated horizontally, caught in a blast of water. Something big was moving near the seafloor.

He peered through the porthole, seeing the exterior lights flash like lightning in a storm. Several yards below him was the station. He could see the north section; a massive spherical cannister connected to a series of tunnels which linked it to the other segments of the station. The exterior lights on the north and east side were still working, providing an outline of the facility's basic shape.

Like clouds passing over the moon, a mass of silt swept from the south side. Mel turned his gaze to the seafloor where it originated. His eyes widened.

"Good Lord."

The faint glow of the exteriors managed to capture the basic shape of the big one. A monster of colossal scale, it had the same basic physiology as its smaller counterparts. Only it was a hundred times their size at least, and a hell of a lot meaner.

It rolled along the seafloor, locked in combat with another large mass. This one was very different in shape and biology. From what Mel could see, the beast lacked limbs, save for a very large tail. Pectoral fins protruded from its torso, serving as wings to help it glide through the sea. During its tussle with the big crustacean, its tail protruded upward, catching some of the glow from the station's lights.

Mel took in its crescent shape. Between that and the rest of the animal's physiology, it became very clear what it was.

"No. It can't be. It's impossible."

The creatures struck the bottom together, resulting in another seismic wave. Finally, the two of them parted. The big crustacean moved northwest toward the mining site, either drawn by the heat or simply fed up with its brawl.

Its opponent righted itself and gently glided over the station, its tail in constant motion. In doing so, its pointy snout angled upward. An ascent began, the tail waving with increased intensity.

Mel's heart raced. It was coming directly towards him.

He looked up at the light glistening from the top of the life pod. A beacon. Meant to alert nearby vessels, it was part of the pod's life preserving system. Instead of rescue, it lured his doom right to his porthole.

Mel shrieked as the leviathan closed in on the pod. Its jaws parted, revealing white teeth the size of daggers.

The jaws slammed shut over the pod. The bulkheads bent, then succumbed to pressure. In the blink of an eye, Mel Haysen was reduced to red jelly. The remains of the pod were spat from the creature's jaws, and settled on the trench floor, scattering among the wreckages of the other escape pods, all of which had suffered the same fate.

CHAPTER 2

Surface Station Guardian.
Pacific Ocean – 1,630 miles west of Ecuador.

"It's gone."

Captain Dennis Kelleway leaned over the shoulder of his radio operator, Ken Ward. "The hell do you mean it's gone?"

Ken put his hands up. "I mean: it's *gone*!" He gestured at the lifeboat monitoring screen. One moment, they had a reading of a life pod deployment. A few moments later, the signal went dead.

It was the *fourth* time this happened.

Dennis shook his head. The whole situation had been steadily going from weird to weirder. They had been monitoring the radio transmissions and digital logs from the *Scarlett Caldera.* Six hours ago, they had logged the receipt of five hundred pounds of trench core rock. Three hours after that, all staff were alerted to the holding station due to strange readings from the rock. Thirty minutes later, bio signs were reported. Thirty minutes after that, the geologists and station biologists took samples from the ore.

Then came the silence.

In the last hour, no transmission or log had been received by the small crew of the surface station *Guardian.* All attempts to make contact with the *Scarlett Caldera* went unanswered. As far as the four-man crew of the *Guardian* was concerned, the *Scarlett Caldera* had gone dark.

The only intermission in the silence was the detection of three life pods. Upon deployment, their EPIRB (Emergency Position-Indicating Radio Beacon) was automatically activated. No notification was given from the station commander, leaving Dennis to speculate the extent of the emergency. Deployment of life pods was no small matter. They were generally held in the event of a full evacuation, or some medical emergency that could not be handled in the station's infirmary.

Less than two minutes after the activation of all three EPIRBs, the signals went dead. In the time elapsed since then, none of the life pods had surfaced. Given the fact that *Guardian* was anchored less than three hundred meters from *Scarlett Caldera,* the pods would have emerged within eyesight. Even so, Dennis had instructed the third crewmember, Palmer, to search the surrounding area with a drone. So far, no luck.

Two minutes ago, a new EPIRB was activated, signaling the departure of another life pod. Like with the other two, the signal ended abruptly, as though the pod itself was sucked into another dimension.

Dennis reached over Ken and refreshed the computer in a vain hope it was nothing more than a technological error. Even as he tapped the key, he knew he was wasting his time.

"Oh, Jesus."

"We're gonna have to alert headquarters," Ken said.

Dennis put a hand on his head and stepped away from the desk. Three days until his rotation was over, not one single problem throughout the entire month until today. It was the age-old lesson about being prepared for anything. Even with that thought in the back of his mind, Dennis had gladly taken this position as a surface station manager. There was not much to the job: maintain communications with *Scarlett Caldera*; relay logs to Headquarters, monitor the weather and ocean currents, deliver supplies with a cable to the station while also using it to hoist cargo, and keep the *Guardian* tidy.

All in all, it was a cake assignment that paid very well. His title of 'Captain' sounded more lucrative than it really was. He only had three men under his command:

Ken Ward, the radio operator; Palmer, the mechanic; and Goro, the submersible pilot.

"Can you access any of the internal camera feeds?" he asked Ken.

"I'll try." Ken tapped a series of keys, bringing up recordings of the *Scarlett Caldera's* security cameras. After a few minutes, he put his hands up in frustration. "No luck. At least, not for anything that's taken place for the last forty-five minutes. Everything up to that appears to have been normal."

"All the feeds are dead?" Dennis asked.

Ken nodded. "Correct. It's as though something has knocked out the transmitter. That, or the facility lost power, but I'd be getting an alert if the power cell was going bad or was otherwise damaged."

Dennis thought for a moment. No way was he going to alert his superiors without having as much information as humanly possible.

"What about the life pods? Don't they have exterior cameras?"

"Negative. They're life pods, not exploratory vessels. They didn't bother putting exterior cameras on their hulls. Some of them have interior cameras, but I haven't been able to get a decent signal from the first three. Just grainy images. I can try bringing up the feed from the latest one."

"Do it."

With Dennis hovering over his shoulder, Ken brought up the file with the feed from Lifeboat A-3.

"Okay, I've got something."

Dennis leaned forward to watch the screen. They saw a single individual hurrying into the lifeboat. He watched through one of the portholes for a minute or so, hands shivering.

"That's Mel Haysen," Dennis said. "He's one of the geological experts."

"He looks like he's in a hurry to leave," Ken replied.

They watched the geologist on the screen, both exclaiming as he initiated the launching procedure. The lifeboat began ascending into the topside airlock, its sole occupant keeping his eyes to the glass the entire time.

Before long, he was expelled into the open ocean.

Moments passed, and they witnessed Mel Haysen scream in horror and fall away from the porthole. Next came a massive jolt, and the feed went dark.

Dennis and Ken remained silent for several more moments, absorbing the visual information they had just taken in.

"That settles it," Ken said. "Something's officially wrong. I'm calling Headquarters."

"Go ahead and do that." Dennis stepped to the far side of the office and rummaged through the file cabinets, ultimately locating the station's SAT phone.

Ken stared at him, radio mic in his hand. "You alerting the Coast Guard?"

"For starters," Dennis said. "Something's down there—something that forced several people to attempt evacuation, only to get picked off after deployment. The VPs might object, but I think we need a different kind of specialists to figure out what's going on."

Ken put the pieces together. It was hard to believe, but he could not deny the truth of what he had just witnessed. The Captain was correct; the corporation would resist any assistance. But in the end, he agreed with Dennis. If, in fact, there was something down there killing the crew, sending the company's security forces would only create more victims. Something like this required a group with a particular specialty; someone with experience in unknown dangerous organisms.

"Yes, Coast Guard? This is Captain Dennis Kelleway of the Brom-Caylen Corporation, calling surface station *Guardian*. I am calling for assistance on behalf of the deep-sea mining facility *Scarlett Caldera*, located in the Half-Moon Trench. We have lost all communication, and do know that the staff was in the middle of an unexplained evacuation… No, I don't think it was a hull breach of the station. To be frank, sir, I think there's something down there. I'll send you a file with the footage we have… That's correct: I think this is a job for G.O.R.E. Sector."

CHAPTER 3

G.O.R.E. Sector research cruiser Crixus.
573 miles west of the Galapagos Islands. 43 miles from Surface Station Guardian.

It was a little after zero-seven hundred hours when *Firebird-One* set down on the cruiser's flight deck. The boarding ramp lowered, making way for the leader of Raptor Pack, Captain Thomas Rodney. It was another day ending in Y; another day where monsters threatened human lives. Every day, Thomas woke up with a single mandate: to destroy all monsters and preserve the safety of innocent civilians. Fourteen years of military service and a commitment to both his duty and the people around him fueled his resolve.

Walking beside him was Dr. Charity Black. Her specialty in biology, botany, and several other professions was concealed behind a hardened military exterior, both in attire and attitude. Even out in the middle of the ocean, she was ready for close combat. Experience had taught her that reconnaissance missions were unpredictable and could quickly escalate into an all-out conflict.

The level of threat varied among the mutations. Some were enhanced predators, posing danger to no more than a local area. Others, like the wasp and hornet invasions that led to Thomas Rodney's first collaboration with the team, could potentially escalate to an extinction-level event.

Their common trait: *every* mutation was dangerous, and had to be exterminated. It was their curse, as none of the subjects asked for this fate. All of them were normal everyday animals, living out their lives, until the fall of the Ecclesiastes Intergalactic Meteor Storm of 2019 corrupted their DNA structure and transformed them into a sinister version of themselves, and put them on a path of violence.

Compassion for the mutations was limited to the heart. It was not part of the job description.

Nobody understood this better than Sergeant Ray Archer. He stepped off *Firebird-One,* a grenade launcher strapped over his left shoulder, and a Pterosaur-EM sniper rifle secured in his hands. Right away, his eyes went to the surrounding ocean. As far as he was concerned, the threat could be right under the ship this very moment. His singular purpose was to seek it out and destroy it without hesitation nor mercy.

Then there was Lieutenant Renee Larson. After shutting down the MEAV's engines, she followed her teammates onto the ship's deck. In her hand was a travel mug—an *empty* travel mug. In the mind of G.O.R.E. Sector's ace pilot, the only thing worse than a deadly monster invasion was running out of her beloved pumpkin spice coffee. She did not wait for the appropriate season for the beverage, because Renee's opinion was *all year round* was the season for pumpkin spice.

Pumpkin spice, and killing monsters.

The research cruiser was nothing like the naval warships utilized by G.O.R.E. Sector, and was less than half the size of the *Jack Arnold.* However, it was not without its defenses. In addition to the Bushmasters autocannon on the forecastle, machine guns and grenade launchers were installed on the bow, stern, and middeck areas of the vessel. Small arms were stored in the ship's armory, providing the crew with a variety of rifles, pistols, and RPGs.

As with most of G.O.R.E. Sector's missions, there was always a squadron of jets and helicopters on standby. In light of the public's awareness of mutations and the dangers posed, funding was quickly approved for more air and air bases throughout the world operated specifically for the functions of the Sector. It was a question of diplomacy, as many countries viewed it as an excuse for the U.S.A. to post more military bases on foreign lands. The American public had its fair share of debate, with many internet and television personalities questioning the true motives of G.O.R.E. Sector and the use of its funds.

It was a verbal civil war which kept the expanse of the organization at a snail's pace. The secrecy prior to the insect invasion in Oregon fueled the public's apprehension. In spite of what officials claimed, most people understood that government secrecy usually meant something shady was going on behind the scenes.

Thomas Rodney could not blame anyone for such feelings. On the very first day, General Austin Kilmore had let it slip there were powerful individuals, some even in the U.S. government, who wanted to exploit the mutations for their own benefit.

That issue was front and center on his mind today. Usually, it was public areas that were at risk of mutant contact. Today was a change, as it was not a nation requesting assistance, but an employee of a large organization called Brom-Caylen.

An *employee*, not the company heads. In fact, when people in G.O.R.E. Sector attempted to reach out to their headquarters in Hawaii, they were told there was no emergency and asked to stand down. Yet, the surface station manager remained adamant that something was going on in their deep-sea facility. There were no signs of significant damage to the structure's integrity, though external sensors had detected some unexplained abnormalities. The comms system and security surveillance system were down. All they had was some alarming interior footage from one of the life pods. The fact they were even being deployed was concerning in itself; the fact none of those pods made it to the surface was enough to get Raptor Pack out there.

On the main deck of the G.O.R.E. Sector research cruiser, they beheld the sight of the deep-sea Star-Class submarine *McQueen*. It was thirty feet from bow to stern. Like the Journey-class submersibles, it was designed to descend to depths of five miles, and like the Mako combat subs, they were equipped with electric shock-tipped harpoons, mini-torpedoes, and flares. Unlike most DSVs, it was agile even under extreme water pressures.

Standing beside it was the man who invented the machine, and the fifth member of Raptor Pack. Dr. Howard Tate was using a pistol-shaped scanner to comb the *McQueen's* hull with a green laser in what was probably the thousandth round at checking its integrity. He had traveled to the cruiser separately, having needed to take a detour in order to collect the DSV.

He lowered the scanner and turned to face his teammates. "Hey guys. How the heck did I beat you here?"

"Good morning, Howard," Thomas said. "We had to make a quick detour in Cambodia. They had a case of worms."

Howard bit his lip. "I suppose it's safe to assume they weren't the kind you could put on a fishing hook."

"Given some of the fish that might be out there, I'm sure we can invent a hook big enough," Thomas said. "Anyway, it proved to be a relatively simple matter for a change. We hit the ground with an electric current, brought them to the surface, and torched them with flamethrowers. Didn't even take an hour."

"Thanks to me," Charity said, proudly pointing a thumb at herself. "Ol' Army Man here wanted to organize a big crossfire and storm the nest of worms as though we were invading Normandy. Luckily, some of us believe in working smarter, not harder."

Thomas grinned. "Being from the Chair Force, it comes as no surprise 'work harder' is a difficult concept for you to grasp."

He got the punch in the arm he anticipated, and the chuckling from Howard and Renee.

Archer, as usual, remained stone-faced. Some things never change.

"We'll arrive at the destination in approximately two hours," Howard said. "Unfortunately, I'm still not sure what it is we're dealing with. If anything."

"It's definitely something," Thomas replied. "The captain of the surface station is risking his job by alerting us. The heads of the company probably don't want prying eyes into whatever operations they've got going on down there."

"Brom-Caylen Corporation," Howard said. "They're pioneers in weapons manufacturing, energy research, and deep-sea exploration." He shrugged, not leaving anything up for interpretation. "I did some work for them during my Navy service, constructing designs for large facilities to operate in deep underwater locations. *Scarlett Caldera,* while I wouldn't call it my baby, I did have a hand in it."

"What do you know about the company?" Renee asked.

Howard crossed his arms. "They like to have influence."

"Irvin Brom, in particular," Thomas said. "I did a little homework on him during the ride over. His empire supposedly had humble origins back in the early 2000s, with a food distribution company of all things. Next came food production. Out of nowhere, he was buying up all kinds of farmland. There was more than just cows, pigs, and chickens on those properties. He invested all sorts of money in technology. From there, he designed pharmaceuticals for animals, many of which are used by veterinarians today. And, of course, there were new techniques on growing food. Meat, vegetables, grains—you name it."

"Synthesized foods," Howard said.

Charity's face contorted into a look of disgust. "I feel like I'm getting cancer just picturing that."

"Oh, don't worry, he's been working on that too," Thomas said. "Not a cure. Oh no. But new therapies and treatments."

"And Yohan Caylen has tendrils in multiple insurance companies," Howard added. "The point is, they're an empire, and steadily expanding. They're not as in-your-face as other companies, but they like to pull strings from the shadows. You think those labs are just for food and medicine?"

Charity shook her head. Experience with the human species from all over the globe had enabled her to read the fine print.

"They're conducting experiments," she said.

"Now they're meddling with energy," Howard said. "You know, sustainable energy. Everyone wants it, but every time we come close to a solution, there's always some sort of setback. For nuclear, people are still afraid of meltdown incidents like Chernobyl. For fusion, many people are worried about containment and waste, not to mention a lack of tritium."

Renee perked up. "Wait? Tritium is real? I thought that was just invented for *Spider-Man 2*."

Howard glared at her. Of course, Renee had to get her pulp culture reference in.

"Yes, it's real, Lieutenant."

"They're also involved in weapons manufacturing," Thomas said. "I spoke with General Kilmore about it. It's believed they are supplying materials to several governments and organizations all over the globe. Even the U.S. military in some cases. It's enough to get several congressmen and senators to play interference on the company's behalf."

"G.O.R.E. Sector doesn't use them as suppliers, do they?" Renee asked.

"No, we use a rival of theirs," Howard said. "It's a smaller company, but they have access to the metals we use for drones, vehicles, and other technologies. As for the manufacturing, I can gladly tell you that's being done in the good ol' U.S.A. by G.O.R.E. Sector itself. With the occasional inspection by yours truly, of course."

Everyone took notice of the twinkle in Howard's eye as he said that last part. He was the brilliant scientist version of a kid in a sandbox, and the taxpayer was funding his playtime. Thankfully, that playtime produced useful results.

Thomas took a moment to admire one of those results.

He had seen the *McQueen* once before. Only now, just hours away from his next mission, did he fully grasp the reality of the kind of trip he was going to embark on.

Renee, as usual, was going to serve as the pilot.

"You feel comfortable behind the wheel?" he asked her. It was a question designed to illicit a response, which it did.

Renee's brow furrowed. "Don't you know me at all, Captain?"

Thomas smiled. "My expertise is closer to Archers; I like to shoot stuff. But I'm savvy enough to know operating machines miles under the ocean's surface is drastically different than playing *Top Gun* in the air."

"With our toys, it won't be *quite* as different as you think," Howard said. "Let's just say, we're a few steps ahead of the guys at Brom-Caylen in this regard." He knocked his fist on the hull. "It's designed for infiltration and evacuation. In a limited capacity, of course. It can only hold about six people. It works for us, in this case, as we'll be heading down there to find out what's going on with the *Scarlett Caldera*."

"We'll probably have to dock," Renee said. "Thomas said all communications were down, and that it appears an evacuation was taking place."

"We have masks in the event of it being some sort of chemical leak," Howard said. "Although, I don't think that's what happened. There's all sorts of safeguards in the station for such occurrences. Plus, there's the fact that something clearly intercepted the lifeboats after deployment."

"And the structure's still intact? They weren't evacuating because of a risk of implosion?" Charity asked.

Thomas shook his head. "Not according to the guy who called. You saw the footage he transmitted. The guy inside that lifeboat was clearly attempting to get away from something—something *inside* the station—and it wasn't toxic gas."

"How would something enter a watertight facility without breaching it?" Renee asked.

Thomas and Howard looked at each other and simultaneously came to the same conclusion.

"They were digging for something down there," the former said. "They must've brought something through the airlock, whether accidentally or intentionally." His eyes naturally went to Archer's weapon. "On that note, should we board the station and find something we'll have to shoot, am I correct in assuming typical firearms are not the best idea?"

"Especially not the kind we utilize," Howard replied. "Fortunately, I've anticipated this, being the brilliant guy that I am."

Charity closed her eyes and shook her head. "I'm starting to think I liked you better when you were seasick all the time."

Grinning at that, Howard turned around and waved for the others to follow him. "Come this way to get acquainted with your toys. As usual, it is state-of-the-art equipment you won't find anywhere else." He took a minute to glance over at Charity. "Unless you'd rather stand around and pretend you're doing something. Given the Air Force background, I understand how that might sound appealing to you."

Charity's jaw dropped. "What?! Not cool." She looked at Thomas. "Captain, I see you're becoming a bad influence on Raptor Pack."

Thomas replied with an animated smile as he and the others followed Howard into the interior of the ship, where important equipment awaited them in the laboratory.

CHAPTER 4

Scarlett Caldera
Med/Lab, Room N-218.

The rumblings had ceased, as did the screams. For May Dyner and those crouched inside Med/Lab, it was of little comfort. They knew what lurked within the passageways. Worse, they knew what swam outside the hull of the station.

Twenty-four hours was a lifetime in this predicament. They could not stay, nor could they run. And the company was likely unprepared for what was down here. Any rescue attempt would result in more casualties.

On the other hand, there was no way the company would abandon the *Scarlett Caldera.* Too much had been invested in the deep fortress, and there was much to be gained from it. That, and the trench from which its personnel mined.

It was a situation that led May to question her life's choices. She was one of the few who knew the company was looking for more than just rare-earth elements such as copper, nickel, and silver. There was something else down here that interested the company much more. The rare-earth elements they collected, and the precious tritium deposit underneath the deposit, were just a bonus. And a perfect cover story.

She did not think much of it in the beginning. A job was a job. 'What could go wrong?' she figured.

Today, she wanted to smack herself for such a foolish question. Equally as much, she wanted to smack the three people trapped in the section of Med/Lab with her. During the wait, chit-chat was inevitable, despite the fear of what was nearby. May had voiced the question of what they intended to do if they ever got out of this mess.

To her amazement, they all expressed their eagerness to return to work, so long as they received the hazard pay Brom-Caylen promised in their contract. Of course, the contract simply stated injury, or situations of peril in service of the company. They all figured this counted towards the latter. Given the death toll, it better have.

All the same, May had made up her mind. Her colleagues, Moses, Feinstein, and Alexandra, thought she was insane. Certainly, she would get a nice pay raise. The company had its faults, but they argued they knew how to keep their staff appeased. Funny how the sentiment was only shared by those who survived the assignments.

"Listen, not many of us get opportunities like this," Alexandra said.

May gave her fellow miner a glare as cold as the surrounding sea. Ever since the question was brought up, she felt the need to justify her stance. Like many of the people aboard the *Scarlett Caldera*, she was a digger by trade, working in hellish conditions using equipment that was barely passable. Mineral mines across the country faced similar hazards. On-site accidents, exposure to dust and chemicals, demolition accidents, among other problems. Down here, there were a fair share of risks, but at least the equipment was up-to-date, and the pay was much better. Hell, Brom-Caylen was one of the few private companies that offered pensions these days.

On top of that, she was certain rescue was on the way.

May could not dispute that last part. Again, it was a question of whether the rescue party was sufficiently prepared. She had heard that the comms were not working, or at least Operations failed to get a response from the *Guardian*. She had felt the vibrations up top. It would not come as a surprise if she learned the antenna tower had been destroyed.

"Don't worry about it," May said. "It's your choice."

Alexandra put her arms around her knees. It was amazing that someone with such a petite build could handle one of the drilling suits. To Alexandra's credit, she rocked the equipment as well as Moses, who was a miner of six-foot-four with arms that looked as though they could move the underwater mountains all by themselves.

"Don't act like you're not judging me," she said.

May put her head against a cabinet and reminded herself not to take the bait. Alexandra was not a bad person by any means. Tension had a way of making people behave erratically. She had seen several of her friends slaughtered at the hands—or rather, claws—of those things. Furthermore, the station administrators pretty much said 'to hell with everyone else' and jumped ship. Those lifeboats could easily hold six people each. Maybe eight.

She had heard one of the implosions from the submersible pool. For her, it was an unmistakable sound. Working three miles deep, one quickly learned what every vibration meant. She had also gotten a glimpse of the large shapes through one of the portholes.

That big one, and whatever else was out there, were quick to respond to water distortions. For them, the lifeboats were easy prey, especially since the ascent was relatively slow. If one was taken out, it was a safe bet to assume the others did not make it either.

"You do what you think is best," May finally said.

Alexandra shifted, nearly succumbing to the urge to argue.

Feinstein, a pudgy man with a black beard and pores almost as large as the Half-Moon Trench, stood up. "I could go for a bite to eat."

It was a statement that managed to get May to smile. Even with hell having broken loose, the guy still had food on his mind.

"Eating's for the living, right?" she quipped.

The SeaCAT operator shrugged. "Makes sense to me." He stood up and moved across the small room to the minifridge. It was to their benefit that the doctor and nurse on station tended to take snakes from the galley and store them in here. Their work required long rotations in the office, and they determined it was beneficial not to have to make trips to the mess hall. Plus, the workers often left it a mess.

May could not begrudge the sentiment. The people aboard the *Scarlett Caldera* were good, blue-collar workers, with mostly honorable lives, but many were undeniably slobs who had a toddler's sense of cleaning up after themselves.

Still, none of them deserved what happened yesterday.

"We all know what they wanted us to dig for down here. The whole spiel about sustainable energy makes for a good headline. Makes the company look good. Makes *us* look good. But what's under that mine… we can't let them have it."

"It's not up to us," the hulking Moses said. "If not Brom-Caylen, it'll be someone else. Maybe even someone worse, who will use the stuff for illicit intentions."

May scoffed and looked over at him. "What other intentions would they have with the stuff? You think anything good can come from it? It's clear to me what anyone would plan to use it for. And what happened down here was just an *accident*. Unplanned, and in a relatively isolated area. Imagine if one of those 'things' got loose topside. On that note, I think it's fair to say they'll eventually make it topside. I saw what was in the mine when we brought the rock in… or, what we thought was a rock."

She shivered, wishing she could turn back time and leave the so-called geo sample in the seabed where it belonged. Better yet, she wished she had planted some underwater charges on it and blew the damn thing up.

Alexandra got up and joined Feinstein at the fridge. She was not interested in food, but rather the water bottles. She had to be careful not to drink too much too quickly. There was no telling how long they would be trapped down here, and their rations would only last so long.

Feinstein, having swallowed eight ounces of water in a few large gulps, tossed the empty bottle in the trash and went around the corner to the small restroom.

Again, there were worse places to be trapped. They had originally come here after Feinstein had suffered a small laceration by one of the insectoids. Fortunately, it proved to be less severe than they thought. For better and for worse, they realized there was no way to escape, for the creatures regularly patrolled the passageways. Maybe they had settled down by now, since the infestation was complete, and there was no other prey other than the four workers.

All the same, going outside this room was too risky.

May endured the sound of Feinstein relieving himself, and heard the inevitable flush. She cringed, as the sound was loud enough to make her nervous.

"Are you trying to ring the dinner bell?" she hissed at her co-worker as he stepped into the lab area.

Feinstein put himself on the single patient bed and crossed his feet. "They haven't heard it yet. At least, they don't seem to care what it is."

He quickly uncrossed his feet and crouched to the floor at the sounds of rigid tapping overhead. The sound moved up and down the bulkheads, the rhythm of vibrations creating a mental image for all four stragglers of the swarm lurking in the air ducts and passageways.

Everyone remained silent, watching the door in fear of it being hacked to bits by an array of claws.

Alexandra moved next to May. In spite of their differences, she had no intention of having her friend get taken without a fight. May put a hand on her shoulder, conveying the same sentiment.

Minutes passed, and the sound gradually subsided.

More minutes passed, during which all four workers waited in dead silence.

Feinstein exhaled slowly. "I'll be more careful next time."

May relaxed and leaned against the bedframe. This was a hell that could not freeze over soon enough. Frankly, she saw no way out of it.

"Someone better come," Alexandra muttered.

"Whoever does come down here, they better be the toughest sons-of-guns to ever walk the earth," May replied. "Fingers crossed."

CHAPTER 5

G.O.R.E. Sector research cruiser *Crixus*.
24 miles from Surface Station *Guardian*.

"*This* is state-of-the-art?"

Howard stood puzzled at Thomas' observation of the Pheonix-M2 Plasma Rifle. The silver-plated weapon was moderately larger than an M4 Carbine, and was similarly weighted. Its frame was slightly wider, and its battery mag an inch longer than a typical thirty-round magazine, but overall, it comfortably fitted in the hands of a soldier.

In fairness, it was not the size Thomas complained about, but the range of its projectiles.

"Listen, not even I can snap my fingers and have *Phase Plasma Pulse Rifles* on hand for you. This is the closest we presently are to that kind of tech. Believe me, this is safer than firing lead projectiles at terminal velocity inside a pressurized structure."

Thomas held the weapon vertically, arms outstretched as though the thing had cooties. Fed up with what he was watching, Howard took the weapon from him.

"It's not gonna hurt you."

"Trust me, I'm not worried about that," Thomas said. "I'm more worried about whether it'll hurt whatever I'm shooting at."

Howard bumped him with the butt of the weapon for that comment disguised as a concern.

"A single plasma bolt from one of these things will burn through your Kevlar and leave a six-inch hole in your chest. Even if you were to somehow survive getting shot, the organs closest to the hit are guaranteed to be damaged by the heat."

"Yes, I heard you the first time you explained that," Thomas said. "The plasma bolts are hot as hell. So hot, they burn themselves out after like two feet."

Howard shook his head and exhaled. "Ye of little faith. They go farther than two feet. But yes, they're fairly short range..."

"How short a range?" Thomas asked.

Howard's lips tightened, as he knew the captain would not like the answer. "They burn out at around eighteen-to-twenty feet." As expected, Thomas soured at that answer. "That's the drawback. Still, they're a safer option down there than armor-piercing rounds."

"Is there a risk of the plasma bolts burning through the hull?" Charity asked.

Howard shook his head. "The metal comprising that station is rated to withstand three thousand degrees. The projectiles burn at twenty-six hundred. Enough to get the job done. The only thing they will hurt is whatever is unlucky enough to be in the crosshairs... within twenty feet, of course."

Thomas looked over at Archer and handed him the weapon. The marksman knew what was up; he was gonna be the one to test Howard's plasma rifle. Thomas grabbed one of the others, and looked at a bunch of paper targets Howard had set up.

A sparkle of glee appeared on the engineer's face. "Ah, yes. I figured you'd want to try them out before we deployed..."

Thomas put a finger through one of the human figures in the paper rectangle.

"I appreciate it, but I want to see how these do on something real." He started looking around the room for a target that would test the killing power of the energy projectiles.

"Well, let's see." Howard started looking around. "We have some welding sheets. Those might be good for—" He bounced on his toes after seeing Thomas turn around and walk towards a white shelf on the opposite side of the room.

On that shelf was a silver dome-shaped helmet with a T-visor.

"This one of your other experiments?"

"No. Not yet, anyway," Howard said. "Actually, I'd like to see if I can make a real-life version of—hold on a sec; I just realized that was not sarcasm, but an honest question. Haven't you seen anything *Star Wars* lately?"

"Not since Episode Eight," Thomas replied with a shudder.

Howard chose not to respond to that and gestured at the helmet. "It's from the Black Series. They make neat replicas, so nerds like Renee and myself can look cool from time to time. I still need to get the *Boba Fett* re-armored one, and the *Darth Vader...* what are you doing?"

Thomas knocked on the thing with his hands. It was pretty solid. Not steel, but still suitable enough to suit his purpose.

"How much did you get this for?"

Howard perked up. Maybe the Captain was interested in getting one for himself.

"I got it for a hundred bucks. But if you—what are you doing?"

Thomas took the helmet off the shelf and went out the door, waving for Archer to follow him topside.

Now Howard knew what was up.

"Don't you even think about it, Captain!"

"I'll buy you a new one. If this thing works, I might even be inclined to get you the *Darth Vader* one."

"Why don't I believe you?"

All the way up, Renee was grinning ear-to-ear. "Too bad it's not made of real *beskar.*"

Thomas and Archer went to the portside gunwale and faced the deck, with Howard standing beside the former.

"Oh, come on, Cap! That livens up the lab and..."

Thomas swung the helmet back as though about to roll a bowling ball, then tossed it high.

Archer took aim and waited for the helmet to return to earth. As it came within the twenty-foot range, he fired off a shot.

A glistening blue ball of hot energy ripped from the muzzle of the gun and struck the helmet, bursting it into multiple fragments of charred and melted plastic and electronics.

Howard dropped his arms and pursed his lips, watching the remains of his collector's item rain onto the deck of the ship.

"Satisfied, now?"

Thomas nodded with elevated enthusiasm. "Indeed I am. Nice work, Dr. Tate."

Howard glared at him. "Glad I could oblige."

"Oh, geez." Thomas dug out his phone. "Like I said, I'll buy you a new one. Thanks to these superphones you provided us with, I have service everywhere. Nice perk of the job. What were these things called? Blackhead helmets?"

"Black *series*," Howard corrected him.

Thomas punched in the words and found the type of helmet Archer just destroyed. He put his eyes to the screen, his face malforming as though he had witnessed a gruesome murder.

"Three hundred dollars?! You said it was only a hundred."

"That was before it went out of stock," Howard said. "That's what I was trying to tell you before. They just ran out, and it's unclear if they're gonna resume production. Until then, we're stuck with third-party sellers."

Thomas groaned. "Three hundred dollars for a glorified bucket. Highway robbery."

"Oh, you're buying it," Howard said. "*And* the *Darth Vader* one."

"I didn't promise that…" Thomas responded.

"Uh-huh. Nice try. Add it to cart and go to checkout." Howard reached over and tapped the button on the screen to speed up the process. "Come on."

"Wait, look," Thomas said, scrolling down at some similar items. "How 'bout one of these instead? They're still in stock for ninety-nine bucks. Look, there's this one. Bo-katten…"

"*Bo-Katan*, and no!" Howard exclaimed. "Last I checked, I'm not a woman. Get that for Renee, instead."

The Lieutenant raised her hand. "I support this! It'll go great with my *Armorer* one!"

Thomas continued his attempts to get off cheap. He scrolled through a couple more options, then pointed at another helmet.

"How about this one?"

Howard facepalmed. "A stormtrooper? Are you for real, Captain? Buy that for Archer. At least it would be ironic, since they can't hit anything and he can shoot the nuts off a fruit fly."

Thomas groaned and conceded defeat. He typed the *Darth Vader* helmet in the search bar and brought it on screen. Once again, he recoiled in sheer horror.

"Four hundred bucks?!"

"Same thing. Out of stock," Howard said. Again, he reached over and pressed the 'add to cart' button to avoid a drawn-out debate. "Should've gone with the welding sheets."

With a look of disgust, Thomas began going through the checkout.

"Wait!" Renee said. "Don't forget to add the *Bo-Katan* one to the cart! And a stormtrooper one for Archer."

Thomas whipped his eyes at her. "What?"

"Might as well add one for Charity," Howard said. "She'd probably be for the *Sabrin Wren* helmet."

"I don't know," the biologist said. "Not sure what that looks like."

Howard snatched the phone from Thomas' hands and pulled up the store page with the helmet. Charity took a look, then nodded with wide eyes of interest.

"Ohh! Very cool! I'm not big into this stuff normally, but what the hell? Yeah, add that to the cart."

Thomas stared blankly, watching his net worth take a nosedive.

The misery only increased with the unmistakable sound of distant rotor blades spiraling on the horizon.

Archer pulled a sniper scope from his pocket and aimed it eastwards. "It's a Chinook. It's hauling some major equipment—a submersible." He passed the scope to Thomas, who quickly took a look for himself.

The huge machine was moving fast. Its hull was painted black, eliminating any military identifiers. It was a privately owned chopper, undoubtedly operated by security staff of the Brom-Caylen Corporation.

"Looks like they're attempting to make a dive of their own," he said.

"I would expect some pushback when we arrive at the station," Charity said. "Something tells me the company reps are going to take the stance of 'we have this covered. We don't need anyone's help.'"

"I'm curious to see if that's the case," Thomas said. "Because that's a multi-billion-dollar facility. One would think they would be glad to have any assistance in making sure it remains intact and its personnel brought to the surface unharmed. The only reason I can figure they would reject our help is there's an aspect to their operation they don't want anyone finding out about."

Raptor Pack watched as the large helicopter passed overhead and continued northwest.

"I guess we'll find out," Howard said.

CHAPTER 6

Surface Station *Guardian*.

After the sighting of the chopper, the *Crixus* went to full-throttle. By the time it arrived at the station, the chopper was on the *Guardian's* helipad, undergoing a refuel while its passengers gathered near the docks on the northeast side. There, two submersibles were moored, one of which was the one hauled by the Chinook.

Howard took pleasure in the sight of the deep-sea vehicle. Despite being considered state-of-the-art in the eyes of most organizations, it paled in comparison to the *McQueen*, or anything else he developed.

When the *Crixus* came near the station, they received clearance from Captain Dennis Kelleway to dock on the west side. There, Raptor Pack boarded the platform while the vessel's crew readied the *McQueen* for deployment.

Dennis' collar was undone and his hair unkempt. Thomas could not help but suspect this was not usually the case for the station supervisor. He was visibly perplexed, not just from whatever was happening three miles below, but also the presence of the company's own response team.

"Thanks for arriving so quickly," he said. "I don't know what's happening down there, but I can say with confidence that it's more than a radio malfunction."

"Understood," Thomas said. "Would you be able to present us with a layout of the *Scarlett Caldera*?"

"Absolutely. Please follow me."

Dennis led the team to the radio shack, where another equally exhausted staff member was slumped in his desk chair, chin on his palm.

"Welcome to the party," he muttered.

"Yippee," Renee replied.

"Pardon me, Ken," Dennis said to the man. He pulled up another chair and began punching a series of keys.

"You know, you have your very own computer on your very own desk," Ken said.

"Yeah, but yours is the fastest. And time is of the essence," Dennis replied. After a few moments, digital files of the *Scarlett Caldera* came up on the screen. The first page showed a broad, exterior blueprint of the facility and its surrounding structures. Next came layouts of its individual floors and sections.

He turned to face Raptor Pack. "We'll get this on a disk for you, and you can study the designs during your descent."

"Sounds good to us," Thomas said. He leaned left to get a glimpse of the personnel on the east platform. Most of them were men in tactical and EMS gear. He got a glimpse of one of the open supply bags they carried. In addition to some tools and medical gear, they had a fair supply of assault rifles.

Lovely.

Thomas counted a total of twelve men altogether. There were others on another part of the platform, dressed in similar attire and openly carrying rifles. Seeing as there were no other submersibles available, it was clear those extra guys were serving as a guard for the surface station. It practically confirmed in Thomas' mind that Brom-Caylen knew more than they wanted to let on.

His eyes went back to the twelve guys on the dock. There was a thirteenth member; a man in slacks and a white button-down shirt and an undone tie. Definitely a company man who rarely had to take a step on the field. He was speaking to one of the military-looking guys, a fella slightly taller than Thomas and probably a lot less friendly judging by the way he glared at the *Crixus* on its arrival.

The two men approached a stairwell which took them up to the radio shack.

"Oh, great," Dennis said. It was the sound of a man who knew he was about to get chewed out in spectacular fashion.

"They didn't know we were coming, did they?" Charity said.

"No, they did not," Dennis said. "If G.O.R.E. Sector has any openings for office staff or anything like that, please let me know. Because I'm probably not gonna have a job by the end of the day."

Thomas wanted to ask what was going on down there the company wanted to keep under wraps, but decided to keep to the topic of the mission at hand.

"What else can you tell me about the Half-Moon Trench?"

"There's a major dig site roughly a third of a mile west of the station," Dennis replied. "The logs stated they brought in a major sediment load through Lift Two, located in West Station, before everything went dark. The miner who helped bring it in objected to bringing the load into the station until further inspection could take place, noting abnormalities. The station administrator denied the request." He glanced over his shoulder to gauge how much time he had until the two men stepped inside. "The trench is a chasm that stretches over five miles. Despite its name, it's more like a crescent moon, but I guess that didn't have as good of a ring to it."

"I suppose not," Thomas said.

Dennis tapped his fingers incessantly on the desk, hoping for the computer to finish getting the information on the disk. The bar slowly filled to a hundred percent, and he ejected the disk and handed it to Thomas, who promptly passed it to Howard.

"Mind acquainting me?" Thomas said, tilting his head at the two men appearing on the deck outside of the shack.

"The suit is Vinnie Gavel. Nothing remarkable to tell about him. He's the stereotypical corporate stooge who sucks up to anyone above him and talks down to almost everyone below him on the totem pole. Only exception to that second part is that guy he's with; Stewart Durell. He's as mean as he looks. He spent time in the Marines. I don't know what his whole history is, but given his position, I think it's safe to assume he did more than work as a recruiter at the mall. Vincent will be the thorn in my ass during this whole ordeal. Durell will be the one in yours."

That point was made perfectly clear the moment those two men entered the shack.

"You guys can get back on your canoe and head back to wherever it was you came from," Durell said. "I see the tin boat you have getting prepped for deployment. It's clear you're looking to stick your noses into our business. Our people have it handled. We don't want you here. We don't need you here. Go away."

Thomas tried not to smile, knowing it would probably escalate this already unfriendly encounter. Still, part of him liked the straightforwardness of the team leader. At least the guy was honest and didn't like to waste anybody's time.

Vinnie Gavel was a little less hostile, though still not exactly friendly. Dennis Kelleway's concerns were confirmed by a piercing gaze from the company man as he stepped inside.

"I appreciate you offering assistance," he said to Raptor Pack. "But, this surface station and the underwater facility *Scarlett Caldera*, as well as all of Half-Moon Trench, is under the ownership of the Brom-Caylen Corporation. As much as we are grateful for the assistance you offer and the fact you were willing to trek all the way out here, I can assure you the situation is under control. That said, any action will be perceived as interference, and will be dealt with by force if necessary. So, please depart."

Now Thomas was smiling. Watching this fella, who sweated in any temperature higher than seventy degrees, trying to sound stern with him.

"This station is not recognized by the American government," he replied. "And the Half-Moon Trench is not owned by anybody. Any government who might support you is Costa Rica, and good luck getting them to challenge G.O.R.E. Sector. By the way, you know that stands for Giant Organism Reconnaissance and Extermination, right? If there's a reported threat of a giant organism, we have to investigate. *Reconnaissance.* It doesn't matter what toys are owned by whom. If there's a mutation down there, it possesses a threat to more than just your people. So, pardon me, but we will be conducting our investigation. Any interference on *your part* will result in multiple American Naval ships showing up before sunset along with a dozen other G.O.R.E. Sector units, all operating under the supervision of General Austin Kilmore. My guys on the *Crixus* will maintain constant communication with my team, and will have direct access to our interior and exterior camera feeds. If any shady business goes on down there, trust me, they'll know."

Vinnie Gavel broke eye contact, trying to invent some sort of recourse in order to save face. Getting talked down to by anybody on a company station was not going to look good on a report. Unfortunately for him, the facts supported Thomas Rodney's threat.

Durell was unfazed. If anything, he developed a new admiration for the leader of Raptor Pack, even if he remained adversarial.

"And, by the way," Howard added. "That 'tin boat,' as you referred to it, can go a mile deeper than those fishing bobbers you have out there, and can move a lot faster. Oh, and it's rated for undersea combat. So, be grateful for our presence, because if there is something dangerous lurking outside the station, we might be your only hope in staying out of its gullet."

Durell cupped his hands over his assault rifle. "So, you're monster hunting, huh?"

Thomas glanced at the gun. "You say that as if it's implausible. Last I checked, deep-underwater rescue did not have use for guns."

"We've had competitive companies who have tried to steal our product and slow down our operations," Durell said. "For all we know, they docked onto the station and killed the crew."

"Sounds like you've got important work going on down there," Charity remarked.

"The world wants sustainable, renewable energy," Vinnie said. "They want fusion reactors, but the proper resources are not plentiful on the Earth's surface. They're in the crushing depths of the sea. I don't see too many people volunteering to dig it out. Do you?"

Thomas wanted to give the company man credit. The statement almost sounded convincing, probably because it was partly true. But he knew to listen to that inner voice of his. Something else was going on down there, and these guys were worried G.O.R.E. Sector would learn all about it.

It was not the time for tough talk. The fact of the matter was that there were people in the *Scarlett Caldera* who were in trouble. And if there was a mutation down there, it needed to be eradicated, or else others would inevitably be in danger.

"Let's hope it's nothing more than a few disgruntled rivals," Thomas said. "Trust me, compared to what we specialize in, trigger-happy tough-guys are easy."

He looked Durell in the eye as he made that last statement. He gave Dennis Kelleway a quick nod, wishing him luck in putting up with Vinnie. Dennis nodded back, thankful for the unspoken sentiment as well as Raptor Pack's rapid response to the situation.

The team returned to the *Crixus*. The submersible was hooked up to the crane and was ready to deploy.

"I suggest you go potty," Renee said to her team members. "This thing is super advanced, but Dr. Tate couldn't have been bothered to install bathrooms, that even the most basic RV would have."

"Oh, for Pete's sake," Howard muttered.

Five minutes later, the machine was hoisted off the deck. The captain of the *Crixus* offered a salute to Raptor Pack as they were swung over the side and lowered into the water. As Thomas had stated in the *Guardian's* radio shack, the crew was on alert, and would be monitoring everything.

The *McQueen* touched the ocean. The cable detached and the vessel was free to dive.

On the other side of the station, the two submersibles operated by Stewart Durell's security team had deployed and were en route to the station.

"How cute," Renee said. "They think they will beat us there if they get a head start."

"Present them with the facts, Lieutenant," Thomas Rodney ordered.

"With pleasure."

She took it down. Over the next several seconds, the natural sunlight dissipated, and the *McQueen* entered a world of darkness and crushing pressure.

CHAPTER 7

"*McQueen* to *Crixus,* oh-nine-three-one; we are at three-seven-six-five. Steady on course. Rate of descent, point-seven-eight."

"*Copy that, McQueen. Oh-nine-three-two.*"

Renee leaned over in her pilot's seat to look at her crew. "Three-fourths of the way there, guys."

Raptor Pack waited silently in the tight quarters of the *McQueen's* passenger cabin. At this depth, they did not want to make any unnecessary noise that could attract any unwanted attention.

Even with room for one more passenger, the spacing was cramped. Even with the advanced technology at the Sector's disposal, there were certain laws of physics they were bound to. The *McQueen* was already pushing the boundaries. Knowing Howard's skill and endless devotion to his craft, there would probably soon be a DSV even faster than the *McQueen* with double the crew capacity. It would be a major asset in deep-underwater research in addition to battling monsters.

Thomas had provided her the layout of the *Scarlett Caldera*. The facility itself was comprised of four main sections. Spherical in shape, they were anchored to the seabed and were connected to their neighbors by round tunnels, resulting in an overall diamond shape. The sections were clearly labeled: north, south, east, west, all of which had four main decks, with a fifth maintenance deck atop of South Section.

An unofficial fifth section was connected south of the South Section by a large tunnel. It was a dome-shaped structure, a third of the height of the spherical structures, but also twice as wide. A storage station, connected to a garage. According to the schematic, it had a pair of overhead doors that would allow for product to be lifted to the surface.

"West and South are the two primary refinery locations," Thomas explained. "Cargo is hauled through a lift on the bottom into a large chamber, where processing begins. They are moved into a horizontal freight tube from South Section to the storage garage, where it is attached to a cable and eventually brought to the *Guardian*, which holds it until a transport is available."

"Looks like each section has at least one umbilical lock," Howard said. "We can attach anywhere. I guess it's a matter of where we'd like to start."

Thomas gave some thought to the known timeline of events. His inner voice repeatedly reminded him of the fact that the transmissions went black shortly after the intake of a payload.

"We'll find out after we get a look at the place. One thing's for sure, I don't think we'll be entering through West Station." He looked at Charity. "Assuming we are dealing with some kind of mutation, what kind of thing can we expect three miles deep?"

"Could be anything," Charity said. "Cephalopods, some crustaceans, various species of fish."

"Would they be able to make it to the ocean's surface?" Renee asked. "I know there's pressure, temperatures, and other factors that make such a large ascent difficult."

"There is that," Charity replied. "But these mutations have often proven themselves to be capable of things most normal species cannot do. Also, keep in mind, there's a lot we don't know about the sea life at that depth. For all we know, a completely undiscovered species is the one that got corrupted by the mineral, assuming it made it to that depth."

"Great," Renee said from the cockpit. "In other words, it could be anything."

Thomas looked to the blackness on the other side of the porthole. Aside from his own reflection, there was nothing to see. The *McQueen* and the two other subs were all traveling with their lights off, conserving as much energy as possible for when they reached their destination.

It was a surreal feeling, coming this deep. He did a little scuba diving in his Army days, and was trained in the Mako combat mini-submarines designed by Howard. But rarely did he ever go more than a couple hundred feet deep. In every experience, he was guided by natural sunlight, and in the case of piloting the Makos, he had the ability to eject to safety in the event something went wrong. But here, the slightest imperfection in the hull would lead to a crushing end.

He trusted the design of the vessel. It was actually rated to go far lower than three miles. All the same, however, it was simultaneously fascinating and frightening for the team captain. The latter feeling largely stemmed from the lack of control over the situation, as well as the uncertainty of what they were getting into.

"Two items on the sonar," Renee said. "Fifty meters above us. Looks like our company friends are moving a little faster than we anticipated."

"They're pushing their subs too hard," Howard said. "They don't want us to get too much of a head start."

"Should I give them a warning?" Renee asked.

Thomas thought about it for a moment, then shook his head. "Negative. Their squad leader, Stewart Durell, is not the kind of guy to take advice from an outsider. Besides, I have a feeling his pilots have already issued warnings, and he's demanding them to hasten their pace anyway. He's probably been given a large sum of money to secure the *Scarlett Caldera*. In his mind, we're in the way of that."

"They still have no chance of beating us there," Renee quipped.

Thomas looked into the blackness again. While he wanted to inspect the area before anyone else arrived, he did not want to be the cause of two terrible implosions. Not that he would be the one responsible—Durell would hold that card—but all the same, if he could prevent it, he would like to. The whole mission of G.O.R.E. Sector was to preserve human life. Even the jerks. Sometimes, people needed to be protected from themselves. Or, in the case of the two subs, from their superior officer.

Thomas had only known Durell for less than an hour, but he already had a good beat on the guy. He was the type to rule with an iron fist. The fact that the two sub pilots were making their fast descent proved they were more afraid of Durell than the risk of implosion.

"Slow it down," he said to Renee. "Open up comms. Let them know we'll give them first chance to dock."

She opened her mouth to protest, but after a moment of consideration, she understood his line of thinking.

"Ah! Sucks to be the good guy, sometimes," she muttered. She opened up a channel and began the frustrating dialogue with the company security team.

Raptor Pack sat quietly in the tight quarters of the *McQueen.* All five team members shared the same bitter sentiment. Hunting monsters was hard in itself. It was even harder when stupid people entered the mix.

CHAPTER 8

The Half-Moon Trench was the stuff of nightmares. The seafloor had been shaped as though some titanic mythological figure had smashed a giant axe into the bottom of the ocean. The walls overlooking the *Scarlett Caldera* were nearly three quarters of a mile high, their sides extremely steep and textured with millennia of wear and tear from the elements and seismic activity. The bottom of the trench was a series of jagged mountains and hills, all made from rock that was as pitch black as the air around it. Only thanks to 3D scans was Raptor Pack able to get a decent look at the place.

That, and the two remaining exterior lights that flickered on the perimeter of the *Scarlett Caldera.*

All five team members remained dead silent, awaiting for the computer to finish its scan. During those few moments, the two Brom-Caylen submersibles, *Revere* and *Corman*, passed them and proceeded to the huge metal structure.

The four sections, almost resembling vases, stood sixty feet high and were roughly two hundred feet wide. Each one served different functions. The easternmost one was home to crew quarters, the mess hall, lounge, with a lower floor dedicated to utilities. The west and south sections were dedicated to mining services and processing.

"The place is still standing," Thomas whispered. "Power is still on."

"That's good and all, but I'm more concerned about the nuclear reactor," Howard said. "I don't like the idea that it may have gone unattended for the last twenty-four-plus hours. Automated systems *should* keep the radiation levels within normal and the temperature regulated, but if there was some sort of interior damage, it's possible it may go critical."

They waited a few more moments. Aside from the *Revere* and *Corman*, there was no motion detected.

Yet, they knew something was down here. The structure was intact, but that did not mean there was not noticeable damage. Numerous dents and abrasions lined the structures. There was no rhyme or consistency to any of the markings, other than they were definitely made by heavy impacts from large objects containing razor-sharp characteristics.

The antenna tower lay in ruins, having been smacked off its original place and ground into the seafloor. The ground around the structures was full of loose rock from formations that had been decimated during the violent event. Then there was the garage structure, which had suffered the most punishment of the entire complex. Its roof had caved in entirely, exposing everything underneath to the crushing pressure. The walls had lost all integrity and had folded in on themselves.

Renee conducted another scan to get a look at the small dome-shaped structure in the center of the four sections. The reactor building was intact, not showing any signs of breaching.

The security teams conducted their own sweeps. Renee kept the channel open to listen in and keep transparency with what everyone was doing.

As expected, Stewart Durell's voice came through the receiver.

"Corman, continue west. I want you to get a visual of the mine and see if there's anything there that may provide an explanation to what happened here."

"Copy that," the *Corman's* pilot responded. The *Revere* finished a slow circle around the complex and began moving to the base of South Section's airlock.

"What would you like us to do, Captain?" Renee asked. "Attach to the same section, or maybe try a different one? Maybe the east?"

Looking at the sheer size of the place, Thomas was currently feeling regret for not attempting to get a larger team down here. Then again, rescue operations this deep were not on the forefront of anyone's mind. Not even G.O.R.E. Sector's. The Journey-class subs only had a crew capacity of four. They were designed for research, not infiltration and extraction.

"How many airlocks are there in the South Section?" he asked her.

"Only two. There's a loading lift, but it can only be accessed from the company's subs," Renee replied. "I wouldn't be surprised if the Durell guy wants the *Corman* to use the second airlock. And I'm not sure if we'll be able to activate the lift. I think only company vehicles have remote access to that."

"Fair enough," Thomas said. "Let the company guys have the south. We'll take the East Section."

"As you wish."

Renee steered the *McQueen* northeast and closed in on the airlock.

"Corman to Revere, we've got a proximity alert. We've got two bogeys moving in... make that THREE! Three bogeys! Coming from the northwest."

Thomas and Renee looked to the sonar screen. Three objects had appeared just outside the station's perimeter ground barriers.

"Those were definitely not there before," Renee said.

The *Revere* was already in the process of docking with South Section.

"Use flares," Durell instructed.

After a count of three, four simmering balls of red light spat from the sides of the *Corman.* Their hellish glow cast a grim illumination over three cigar-shaped objects zeroing in on the vessel.

They were over thirty feet in length, propelled by a crescent-shaped tail which swayed left and right with incredible force. Wedge-shaped appendages protruded from their left, right, and backs. Even in the thick darkness, their primary weapon, rows of two-inch triangular teeth, were visible in the sparkling glow of the flares. Above those jaws were a pair of large round eyes, as black as the ocean around them.

It was a biological identity that could not be mistaken.

Sharks.

Their flesh appeared rigid, like the carapace of a spiny lobster. Dermal denticles, undoubtedly a result of mutation, protruded over an inch from their sides. Moving in unison, they appeared to be part of a pack. That, or they were siblings.

The *Corman* was attempting to circle back. Two of the sharks broke away in pursuit of the lights, believing them to be prey. The third did not bother. It had its eyes on the target and was keen on getting a bite.

"Revere, we're going to need assistance!"

The sub had completed its docking process.

"Evasive maneuvers, Corman," Durell said, his voice lacking any empathy or concern.

The *Corman's* pilot slowly succumbed to his anxiety.

"Thirty yards… ten yards… Brace—"

BAM!

The shark plowed into the submersible. Despite being only a few feet larger, the fish's strength was drastically superior. With ease, it drove the sub into the seabed.

"We've lost a rudder. Ballast controls not responding."

The sub rocked on the rocky ground, the shark's caudal fin slashing high above it while the fish furthered its attempt to bite through the hull. The glow of the perimeter lights provided the dim view of the other two sharks. They gave up on the flares and quickly moved in to join their brethren in its slaughter of the new visitor.

"Son of a—" Thomas moved to the cockpit with Renee. "Looks like we've got to be the good guys."

"Don't know why they don't just put that on the top of the job description," Renee replied. She armed the weapon systems and faced the sub towards the *Corman*. "Hang on. Might get a little bumpy."

It was now when the speed of the *McQueen* was able to demonstrate its speed and dexterity in the deep water. The great machine shot forward at a speed of twelve knots.

Thomas held on to a handle on the bulkhead, keeping himself steady while his pilot did what she does best.

The shark continued ravaging the sub, thrashing its tail as though trying to push through the seafloor into the center of the earth. A torpedo was a no-go for Renee, for it would finish off the *Corman*. A harpoon would have to do the trick.

She switched on her targeting computer. A 3D image of the fish and its steel victim appeared in a dark green light against a pitch-black background. Crosshairs took form above the shark's left pectoral fin.

"Pew! Pew!" She made a few motions with a finger pistol, then took a real life shot.

The harpoon zipped from the *McQueen's* launcher and struck the predator's thick hide. A blue flash from its electric payload flickered like lightning.

Immediately, the shark released the *Corman* and spiraled into a frenzy. It whipped back and forth, confused and agitated from the strange, unfamiliar pain it experienced.

"I can relate," Renee joked. "I rubbed my feet too much on the carpet the other day. Went to grab a door handle, and ZAP! Whew! I was surprised it didn't leave a mark."

The other two sharks circled their companion, studying whether the writhing shark was worth tearing into. A threatening bite from the fish proved enough to warn them off.

After completing a corkscrew turn, the shark's frantic motions ceased. The harpoon fell from its hide and disappeared into the darkness. Pumping water through its gills, the shark circled back and joined the other two. They swam in unison, ignoring the *Corman* completely.

Their point of interest was clear.

"We have an electric charge in our hull?" Thomas asked.

"That's right."

"Good, because I think it's gonna be put to good use."

The trio of sharks' attention was directed to the large sub hovering in their habitat. There was no time spent on figuring out what this craft was. It did not matter to them. If it was in their vicinity, they wanted to destroy it. And preferably eat it.

They did not come in a straight line, but in a formation similar to a pincer movement, with the wounded shark coming head-on while the other two moved in a semi-circular motion, closing in on opposite sides of the *McQueen.*

Renee began evasive maneuvers.

"Hope ya'll took your Dramamine." As she said that, she ascended ten meters and gunned the throttle. The two sharks crossed underneath the sub, and altered course to pursue.

The third member who was moving directly at Raptor Pack had already arched skyward. It closed in with its jaws parted, gums and teeth extending.

Renee banked to starboard, avoiding impact by a few inches. The shark passed by, its caudal fin slapping the tail end of the *McQueen.*

She moved west at twenty knots.

"Crew of the *Corman*, you guys still alive down there?"

"Yes, we're here."

"Alright, stay put. We'll help you out once we get rid of our friends." She looked at Thomas. "We're probably going to have to use a tow cable."

"Can we attach it to their sub without damaging it?" he asked.

"We have a magnetic clamp that'll attach to their hull," Howard called to him. He was breathing heavily and questioning his affections for the ocean. "Then again, we can't do much towing with these guys on our ass."

"Leave that to me," Renee said.

She moved another hundred yards westward, the glow of the *Scarlett Caldera's* perimeter quickly dimming. The sharks remained in pursuit, moving remarkably fast for animals of their size moving under such deep water.

Thomas looked over her shoulder at the instrument panel, studying each button and switch.

"This thing was built for monster hunting. Did we happen to equip it with any decoys?"

"You read my mind," Renee said. She pointed to a switch on her left in the middle of a large red square. "This will deploy a buoy. Most sea creatures will respond to mild electrical signals according to Charity. That, and it has lights which obviously will stand out in a place like this. If the same holds true for our friends, they'll easily abandon us to inspect this thing, hopefully long enough for us to turn around and fire a couple of…"

A new blip on her screen brought her pause. An object equal to the size of the sharks was moving in fast.

"We've got another one," she announced.

Thomas clung to the metal handle while the lieutenant banked to starboard. Midway through the motion, the shark closed the distance. A quick dive of several meters allowed her to avoid the clutches of its jaws.

However, it did put them right in the path of one of the other sharks.

The *McQueen* shuddered violently from an impact near the starboard wing. Alarms went off in the cockpit, warning Renee of a foreign object attached to the hull.

Sub and shark went into a violent tailspin.

"Holy smokes!" Charity exclaimed. "It's actually managing to hold on. We're talking about solid bite power."

Thomas barely heard her, as he was watching at the other blips closing in on their screen.

"We've got another one coming." He crouched. "Brace for impact."

BAM!

The *McQueen* flipped sideways, nearly throwing its passengers out of their seats.

In unison, Charity and Howard gripped their seats and gritted their teeth. Thomas groaned while keeping himself from hitting the overhead. Renee hunched her shoulders and sounded off a "whooooa!" as the sub made its flip.

Archer, true to his personality, sat quietly while chewing on a piece of jerky.

The *McQueen* completed a full spin, settling right side up, bumping its underside against the rocky bottom.

The two sharks thrashed their heads, trying to use their teeth like sawblades to open up their victim's rigid exterior.

Renee moved the joystick, failing to free the *McQueen* from their deadly grasps. It was time to utilize the sub's primary defensive feature.

She reached to her left and hit that switch in the red square.

Blue strobes illuminated the outside.

The shaking intensified for a few short moments, then ceased altogether as the sharks retreated in unison. The two that had bitten the wings moved in large, jerking motions, their senses temporarily fried by the intense shock they had taken through their mouths. Their comrades moved farther away, driven off by the residual charges surging through the water.

It was not long before they were facing the *McQueen* again, not yet ready to give up on their kill.

Renee lifted the sub off the seafloor and put it in reverse. The two sharks were on her targeting computer, pumping water through their gills and regaining their senses.

Red digital crosshairs formed over both predators.

Renee armed two torpedoes and fired.

"Brace for some turbulence, *Corman*," she said into the radio.

It was advice also taken by her teammates.

The torpedoes connected with their targets. A double concussion rippled through the trench, simultaneous with a brief but fiery flash from the projectiles' payloads. Silt and debris expanded from the points of impact, like the dust from two exploding stars.

Within that cloud of debris was a heap of fins, guts, and teeth, all raining down separately.

Two sharks down. Two more to go.

Aside from ascending several yards in response to the blasts, they did not appear to be deterred. Right away, both of them arched over the cloud of silt and blood, and parted their jaws as they came down for a run at the sub.

They moved with remarkable speed that rivaled that of the *McQueen's*.

Renee reversed the sub and targeted the sharks. With the rate they closed in, there was no time for the targeting computer to lock on.

She had to eyeball it.

She manually aimed at the nearest shark and fired a torpedo.

Half a second later, a tremendous *BOOM* raged through the trench. From its epicenter, a new cloud of silt, blood, and body parts rapidly expanded. The two pectoral fins drifted in opposite directions, trailing blood like fumes from a jet high in the sky.

Bounding over the middle of the blast came the creature's snout and upper jaw, fully detached from the rest of its body.

Three sharks down. One to go.

Renee had momentarily lost visual. It was a short moment, for the cloud parted from the force of a thirty-two-foot living projectile jetting through the remains of its companion.

"Whoa!"

She veered to port.

The shark missed, colliding into a rock structure behind the sub. It exploded into a storm of silt and granite chunks. The fish passed through the structure and turned itself around for another attack.

Renee attempted to target the fish, only to abandon the attack due to a rapidly shortening distance. She turned fifteen degrees port and raced past the shark. After sideswiping each other, the sub and its pursuer moved in sharp turns. Like two planes in an aerial dogfight, they studied the other's trajectory and calculated their next attack.

Again, Renee tried to target the shark. And again, it closed the distance too quickly. In a change in tactic, she charged directly at the shark, hand on the electrical barrier switch.

The flash of blue warned the beast, causing it to pass over the vessel.

BAM!

Renee regained control of the *McQueen*, then tapped a few keys on the computer to run a diagnostic.

Thomas watched the glass, noticing a lack of visible electrical charges. "Did you switch it off?"

"Nope…" Renee looked at the digital outline of the vessel and the flashing segment near the top. "It severed the lateral cable."

"The denticles on its skin," Charity said in realization.

Renee turned them around. "Our main line of defense is gone." She located the shark, then groaned in frustration as it had lined up for another run at them.

For the millionth time, it was already too close for their last torpedo. By the time it would hit, the shark would close in to a few yards. The concussive force of the blast would only crack the glass screen if they were lucky. Down here, any imperfection in a barrier was a death sentence.

Renee had to act fast—nothing new in this line of work. She armed another harpoon, aimed manually, and let it fly.

It zipped from its chamber through the black water, straight between those sets of teeth.

The shark lurched, a plume of blood spurting from its mouth. The harpoon had lodged deep inside its throat, deeply embedded in the soft flesh, and was wreaking havoc on its circulatory system with a strong voltage.

It corkscrewed, its body bent into a half-moon shape.

Appropriate way to die down here, Thomas thought.

The seizure continued for another minute.

In the end, the fish settled on the seafloor, the charge having been spent. By then, the shark had gone into cardiac arrest.

Four sharks down.

"Nice shooting, Lieutenant," Thomas said.

"Thank you." She pressed the radio transmitter. *"Corman?"*

"We're here."

"Bogeys are gone. We're heading your way. We'll attach a magnetic tow cable to your hull and bring you to one of the lifts. Are you able to wirelessly connect with the station?"

"Affirmative. Thanks, McQueen. We owe you one."

"Tacos would be nice," Renee replied. She glanced back at Thomas, having anticipated the look on his face. "What? I like Mexican food."

"What *don't* you like?" he retorted.

"Vegan food," she promptly answered. She located the *Corman* and closed the distance.

"Revere to other units. We have successfully docked and are entering South Section. Well done, G.O.R.E. Sector. Appreciate your help."

The team collectively shook their heads and rolled their eyes. That guy Durell almost managed to sound concerned about his fellow men. Moreover, he almost came off as sincere in his thanking of the team.

"Those sharks practically appeared out of nowhere," Renee said. "How the hell did we not detect them? Our scanners have a wide range."

"Interference from the trench?" Thomas suggested.

"No way," Howard said. "This sub's scanners could map a mile of cave."

"There was no reading until we were a few yards beyond the perimeter," Renee said. "Unless they were sitting there waiting, but last I checked, sharks need to swim nonstop to keep water flowing over their gills."

As usual, everyone looked to Charity for clarification.

"Not every species," she said. "Nurse sharks and wobbegongs can pump water through their gills while in rest. Given the environment, it makes enough sense those sharks had adapted to doing the same thing. They were probably concealed within the rocks and emerged after sensing us."

"Good enough of an explanation for me," Howard said. "Let's just hope that's all we have to deal with down here."

The *McQueen* was now directly above the *Corman.*

Renee deployed the tow cable. Like a fishing line, it extended from the sub to its disabled counterpart. The magnet made contact with the hull. Renee reeled in the slack until the cable was taut.

"Hang on, down there. You might feel like a wrecking ball while we head over to East Section."

She put more power into the rudder and pointed the bow upward. For a moment, it felt as though the *McQueen* was anchored to the trench. The *Corman* shifted a little, then a little more, Renee gradually adding more power. It lifted off the bottom and swayed gently on the cable. The *McQueen* juddered from the weight, the cargo larger than anything it was typically designed to lift.

Slowly but truly, they neared the *Scarlett Caldera.*

"*Corman?* You make contact with the lift controls?" Renee asked.

"*It won't activate until we're close.*"

"Gotcha. Bear with us. We'll get you there."

"*No complaints here. What kind of tacos do you like?*"

Renee chuckled. "As our captain says, there's not much I'd refuse. Thank God this job keeps me active, otherwise I'd probably weigh about three hundred pounds."

The levity was swiftly ruined by a new blip on the screen.

"New proximity contact," Thomas alerted the others. He and Renee stared at the screen. "Is that…"

"Bigger," Renee answered the incomplete question. "A lot bigger. And fast."

Thomas looked at the station. It was so close, yet seemed so far away. Especially East Section, where they intended to dock.

The bogey was five hundred meters out. Judging by its speed and direction, it was definitely coming directly for them. Furthermore, Thomas was able to do the math.

"We're not gonna make it to East Section."

"Nope," Renee said.

"Can you do South Section?"

She shook her head. "Not with the *Corman* in tow."

Thomas groaned. There was only one solution. He pulled the radio's speaker mic off the console.

"*Corman,* we've got incoming. Connect with West Section's lift. It's our only chance."

"*Copy that.*"

He was relieved to get no complaints or questions. At least the guy on the radio had his head screwed on right.

Renee pushed the submersible to its full speed. The engines groaned and the rudders swirled as though intent on butchering the entire ocean.

West Section drew closer and closer.

"Bogey's at two-fifty," she announced. "Speed increasing."

"We're gonna have to use that decoy," Thomas said.

"Once the time is right," she replied.

"Corman to McQueen. I've connected with the lift controls. Lift will be activating in eight seconds."

"Copy," Renee said through clenched teeth.

Eight seconds was a lifetime in a situation like this.

The bogey closed within a hundred meters.

One hundred quickly became eighty.

Eighty became forty.

Renee launched the decoy.

From a tube in the *McQueen's* topside, a large cannister jetted into the open sea. A large red balloon inflated. Strobing lights flickered from the base of the cylinder-shaped unit. Like a weather balloon, it drifted in the wake of the machine that had launched it.

In its glow was the oncoming fiend.

Thomas and Renee watched it through the rear camera monitors, their teammates getting a look through one of the portholes.

It was a beast they were already all-too-familiar with. Unfortunately, compared to what they were looking at, the ones they had dealt with up until now were angels.

A shark.

A *big* shark.

"Of course," Howard moaned.

"Mommy's here, and she's pissed," Renee exclaimed.

"More like she's claiming her kids' meal," Charity said. "Sharks don't form emotional attachment…"

"Science lesson later, Doc," the lieutenant said.

The fish stopped near the decoy and circled it once.

Ahead of the *McQueen,* West Section's lift extended from the underside. It stretched the length of the support beams around it and ignited the white interior lights for the incoming vessel.

"This is gonna be rough," Renee warned those inside the *Corman*. She lowered the sub until it was nearly touching the bottom. For the sub they towed, it bumped viciously as it was literally dragged to safety.

The *McQueen* entered the loading bay.

Renee put the winch to full power. The *Corman* scraped against all sorts of rock formations, marking its hull until it reached the edge of the ramp.

Behind it, the mother shark had spewed out the recently consumed decoy and made her run towards the lights.

"Shut the door!" Renee shouted into the radio.

"I'm trying! I'm trying!"

The door slowly lifted.

Everyone watched intently, cringing as the deadly fish came within a few meters of the doors.

The lift ascended into the section.

BAM!

The entire station vibrated from the heavy collision.

As the water drained and the bay pressurized, the members of both subs caught their breaths.

Howard leaned his head back and closed his eyes.

"I need a vacation."

CHAPTER 9

After the completion of the pressurization process, the loading lifted the two submersibles into the storage compartment. Raptor Pack beheld a sight that was at once spectacular and horrifying. The engineering of this underwater factory was extraordinary, with processing equipment and storage containers throughout. Protective suits for handling the tritium were displayed within a glass chamber near the entrance. The walls were bronze in color; the equipment itself a cross between an indoor construction site and manufacturing facility.

Everything else was red and black—the former being blood.

The five team members remained silent and still, except for their eyes, which glossed over every inch of the processing station in search of movement. Much of the expensive equipment was deformed, knocked out of place, and in some cases, coated with a bizarre brownish fluid.

Several overhead lights were shattered, the ones that remained functional illuminating a vast series of strange markings in the steel ceiling. The conveyor belt had been severed near the east outtake airlock, where it would be transported to the garage. One of the cranes had lifted its arm to its highest point and had swung into the piping system near the north bulkhead. Its operating cab had a glass frame which had been shattered. The levers were bent out of proportion and smothered with blood and grime.

Whoever had operated it was not clumsy, but was attacked at his station.

"I don't think sharks did this," Renee whispered.

"Nope." Charity dabbed her face with a rag, dreading the fact she would be exiting the safety of the *McQueen.* "This was something *way* different."

The moment she dreaded arrived. Thomas shouldered his Pheonix-M2 Plasma Rifle and moved to the hatch.

Archer was right there, waiting to be given the order to take point.

"Look alive, Raptor Pack," the captain said. He looked over at Renee for the results of the computer's scan.

"Radiation levels normal. We're safe." She cleared her throat. "In that regard, at least."

Thomas nodded at Archer.

The hatch door hissed and lifted. Archer moved out and combed the immediate surroundings with the muzzle of his rifle. Confirming the lack of an immediate threat, he waved for the rest of the team to follow.

All five members of Raptor Pack exited the sub and took firing positions near the bow.

Thomas' eyes turned to the *Corman.* The six men exited one-by-one through the tight exit, and formed two firing lines. After a few moments, one of their members approached Raptor Pack.

He was a man in his early thirties, with short, thinning hair, and a HK416 rifle pointed low.

"Corporal Sean Regal," the man said. "Nice to put a face to you guys. I'm the one you've been communicating with on the radio. Thanks for getting us out of that jam."

Thomas shook his hand. "My pleasure, Corporal. I see you all are okay."

"Thanks to you," Sean replied. "If we make it topside, I've some choice words to share with Durell."

One of the guys behind him laughed.

"Yeah, I'd love to see that."

Sean shrugged, then nodded slightly in acknowledgement of the implied intimidation felt towards Durell. He pointed his thumb at his men and introduced them to Raptor Pack.

"The joker with the sleeveless vest who thinks he belongs in a biker gang is Laurie. The short guy with the button nose is Brian. One with the curly grey hair is Spencer... don't let the color fool you; he's barely older than me. Omar's the big one who reminds us all of Bill Duke. Last, but not least, is... actually *named* Duke, though he's a little more like Walter Brennan than John Wayne."

Thomas saw Duke's toothless smile and understood the reference. He tilted his head at his crew to give a quick introduction.

"Archer, Renee, Charity, Howard." He didn't waste time explaining backgrounds and specialties. Sean seemed smart enough to trust they knew what they were doing.

More importantly, he felt the same tingle running down his spine as Thomas did. They were standing in an advanced facility which housed nearly eighty personnel. Now, it was silent, with signs of a horrible aftermath directly in front of them.

"Until we regroup with Durell, my team and I will follow your lead, if you're fine with that," Sean said.

"No problem," Thomas replied. He took notice of the facial expressions on Sean's team members. Clearly, they did not seem fond of what was just said, but lacked the authority to challenge it. Even after everything that happened, they were still worried about getting on Durell's bad side. As far as the captain was concerned, Durell's temper and ego were the least of their problems. "Run a sweep of the processing station. Find any traces of what we're dealing with. And watch your backgrounds when using those guns. I'm not fond of getting crushed into the size of a raisin because of a hull breach."

Sean took a moment to eyeball the special weapons carried by Raptor Pack. In a display of his good judgement and common sense, he assumed they were using something more proper for the occasion and didn't bother asking questions.

"Move out, guys. Secure the area. Duke, get to the tunnel and see if you can open it."

The company response team fanned out and initiated their sweep.

Meanwhile, the five G.O.R.E. Sector personnel set their focus on a large rock near the northwest end of the assembly line. It was still hooked up to a crane cable, and showed signs of processing.

"That's not tritium," Charity said. She inhaled deeply, showing a sudden onset of fear as though staring at the jaws of some horrid leviathan. "That's mineral."

"Not just any mineral, I assume," Renee said.

"What kind of mineral would they harvest from down here that would require protective gear and air-tight sealable containers?" Charity said.

That statement drew Thomas' eyes to the gear scattered around the rock. All of a sudden, he picked up on what she was getting at.

"Wait a minute…"

They approached the rock. Its center was hollowed out, with bits of granite scattered far across the station, as though a small explosive had gone off within the rock.

A series of markings and small indentations extended from the sample and went in different directions. There were many of them, and had it not been for the keen eye of Ray Archer, the various paths would not be so easily identified.

"Something… a lot of somethings… came out of here," he said. He took a minute to study the trails and their trajectories. "Whatever they are, they walk on multiple legs."

"Oh great," Howard moaned. "Bugs?"

"Yes, bugs." Charity sighed and shook her head. "Bugs, three miles *underwater.* And G.O.R.E. Sector only recruits the best and the brightest."

Howard pursed his lips. "Well excuuuuse me. A crab or a lobster, then. Happy?"

She shook her head. Being in this deep-sea coffin with a bunch of crustaceans with rigid exoskeletons was not something she considered a good time.

"They deliberately brought the rock into the station," Thomas said. "I highly doubt they thought it contained tritium."

"Whatever it is, they certainly didn't expect some visitors to burst out of it," Renee said.

"The real question is what they were after to begin with," Thomas said. He noticed the discarded gloves, tools, and storage cubes scattered on the floor. Some of them were made of bullet-proof glass and contained forest-green fragments of the rock. "Charity? You know more about geology than me, but I'm getting a feeling in the back of my neck that's telling me this is not part of the underwater rock." She slowly backed away from the fragment, having come close to making the mistake of touching it.

"Oh, my God."

Renee swallowed. "Is that an 'oh my God, this is really cool'? Or an 'oh my God, this is really bad'?"

Charity exhaled sharply. "It's an 'oh my God, this is *very* bad.'" She looked at Thomas. "I think this is a meteor fragment."

"You can tell that by looking at it?" Howard asked.

"I know because of what's *in* it, aside from the lifeforms that burst out," she said. "I had studied samples attained in meteor landing sites in Fiji and in Antarctica—meteors that came down during the storm of 2019."

Thomas' heart jumped into his throat.

"Wait… you obtained sizable samples of the particle? It wasn't just grain-sized fragments landing everywhere?"

"That's correct," she said. "So much for you being the detective. You didn't do your homework."

Thomas rolled his eyes. "Yes, I didn't read every single one of the eight hundred files I received when I took the job." He pointed at the rock. "You're telling me this is a meteorite full of the monster-making element?"

She nodded. "A *fraction* of a meteorite, based on the texture of the side. It's hard to know for sure."

Thomas looked at all of the green mineral. Given what a small particle was capable of creating, he could only imagine the monstrosities that would result from exposure to several pounds, or even tons, of it.

More alarming was the fact that Brom-Caylen clearly knew about it and were deliberately extracting it.

He looked across the station at Sean Regal. "Corporal! Come over here, please."

Sean jogged over to their location. "We're trying to get the door open. Seems like the station is only running on auxiliary power. Seems the main computer tried to initiate an automatic shutdown of the reactor. The place is running literally on batteries at the moment."

"Hopefully big ones," Renee said.

Thomas stood like a father who had caught his son in an illicit act. Based on the way Sean was looking at the meteorite fragment, he knew precisely what was on his mind.

"I guess now you know why the boss was good with you docking at East Section."

"So, you know about this?" Thomas said. "How long has this been going on? Given how long it must've taken the company to construct this place, I imagine a while."

Sean had the face of a man who was undergoing a hundred different thoughts at once. Thomas knew the dilemma. The guy was grateful for having been saved by Raptor Pack, but still had a fear of revealing company secrets which he very likely had to sign an NDA for.

"This was not about tritium, was it?" Charity said in an effort to speed the conversation along.

Sean slowly shook his head. "I mean, we did find a small deposit... enough to make the cover story work.

Plus, we found copper and nickel down here, so what little public attention the *Scarlett Caldera* got went unquestioned. But, yes, they tracked down all known meteorite landings that occurred in 2019. They discovered that a large one had crashed down around here."

Thomas began to pace. He breathed in through his nose and out through his mouth, conserving his energy and not waste it on lost tempers.

During his first meeting with G.O.R.E. Sector, General Austin Kilmore had explained to him of the dishonest intent of several government officials regarding the particles, hence their desire to keep all knowledge of all mutations secret from the public. A company like Brom-Caylen undoubtedly had deals with elected officials. Such things were usually a 'you scratch my back, I'll scratch yours' sort of thing. The government could not directly use tax dollars to fund their projects. They needed someone with the tools and the ambition to do the dirty work.

Howard ran his hand over his face, fed up with the never-ending merry-go-round humankind was always riding.

"Nothing sells like war."

"When you can't use nukes, use mutants," Renee added.

"Create a mutation, develop a way to control it, unleash it on an enemy," Charity surmised. "Only the stupidest of the stupid would think they would survive the first step."

Thomas took another look at the markings on the floor and bulkheads. "Karma hit hard this time." His eyes went to an open air duct in the wall, where many of those markings led to. "They brought in more than just rock and Ecclesiastes minerals."

CHAPTER 10

"Uh-huh… Copy that… Act like you've said nothing." Durell placed his private communicator in his vest pocket and turned to face the second-in-command of Revere Team, Urich. "Boot up the comms center in this section. I need to get a link to the *Guardian*."

"You don't want to go to North Section?" Urich asked.

Durell shook his head. "I don't believe we're going to be here that long."

Urich, reading between the lines, nodded and jogged off to access South Station's long-range radio station.

In the meantime, Durell took in the aftermath of the deserted South Section's processing station. It was deserted, with signs of a horrible chaos that had swept through the *Scarlett Caldera*. Dried bloodstains marked the deck, bulkheads, and equipment. But there were no bodies, nor were there any remains left to be seen.

Not human, at least.

Two of his six team members, Hiram and Gates, stood over a large yellow pool of dried fluid. Near it were shards of black, rigid material that was neither metal nor granite. They were a little over a centimeter thick and very tough.

From that pool was a trail of yellow droplets which led several yards to a pool of what was definitely human blood, now brownish red from exposure. There, a shotgun lay on the deck with all shells having been fired. Near the east bulkhead was a nine-millimeter Beretta, with most of its magazine spent, plus one empty one laying on the deck near the weapon itself. Like with the shotgun, there was no body. Just blood.

Only the security guys had access to the firearms, and most of them were contained in North Section. Either these guys were responding to something, or were holing up in here. There was no cargo in the processing station at the moment, and according to the logs, the area was only undergoing a cleaning before everything went dark.

With that in mind, plus the way some hand tools were scattered near the bloodstains, it suggested several people had attempted to take refuge here. The tools were in locations where they served no purpose, indicating to Durell they were being used as melee weapons to fend off whatever had chased the staff into the station.

Plus there was the fact that Corman Team had located the fragment. Based on everything the contact had privately informed Durell of the area, it was safe to assume something had accidentally been brought inside with the sample.

"It's up and running," Urich said.

Durell marched over to the processing station's managerial desk, passing the other three team members—Roland, Wynorski, and Petri—along the way. Almost all of the guys lacked personality when on the job, making them barely distinguishable from one another. That was the way Durell liked it. He did not have much patience for nonsense such as personality quirks. The guys were hired for a job, not to be pals. When assigned to him, they all liberated themselves of their individuality and became killing machines who followed every command. Rarely did anyone make the mistake of getting on his bad side, hence Corman's team member making sure to alert him of the situation.

He arrived at the computer. Urich stepped away from the seat and directed him to the transmitter.

"It's hooked up to the mainframe. Should have no problem getting a direct signal topside. It's possible the *Revere's* radio could have gotten through."

Durell shook his head. "The hull on this station is thick. Hard for radio signals not connected to the station's frequency to get through. Besides, I want a private line of communication. Something our 'friends' in West Section can't track."

Urich nodded and joined the others. They exited out the north doors and ascended to the upper levels to secure the rest of South Section.

Durell placed his headset on and made his call.

"Omega-Niner-Two-Eight here. Get the old man on the horn... I don't care what he's doing right now. I need to speak with him this minute."

***

Thomas stood beside Sean at the north stairwell door, waiting for Howard to override the security measures from the managerial computer station. Everyone stood in awkward silence, unable to go anywhere until the doors were opened.

"Heck of a tech expert," the captain quipped to the commander of Corman Team.

The group of guys chuckled.

"Ah, yes, making Dr. Tate the butt of another joke," Howard said. "It's become a staple of working for G.O.R.E. Sector."

He got back to typing.

Everyone waited in awkward silence.

Charity was watching the marks near the air ducts. "In all seriousness, I don't think those doors were meant to be opened."

Thomas looked at the marks and connected the dots. "Whatever was in the rock, they were trying to contain in here."

"And they did a good job," Howard said. "The station's main computer performed what's called a Protocol Twelve shutdown. Basically, that's only enabled when they don't want anything coming out of here. Though, I doubt they were thinking foreign entities. More likely, they were probably worried about a hazardous outbreak from the particle or radiation from the tritium. In a Protocol Twelve shutdown, these doors *can not* be opened from inside. Only outside."

"What?" the security officer Omar said with a deriding chuckle. "In case the rock tried to punch in the access code and contaminate the rest of the station?"

Howard shook his head and looked the tough-as-nails commando in the eye. "In case a *contaminated* person tried to escape." He tilted his head at the shreds of clothing and bloodstains near the exits.

Omar responded with a dull "mmm."

He understood the implication. There were still workers in here when they locked the doors. The only other reaction it got from him was a nonchalant shrug. *Sucks for them, I guess.*

Howard tried a bypass, then gave an exasperated sigh.

"There's no way around it. The other guys are gonna have to open it for us."

Spencer blew raspberries. "Hell of a start to our sweep. At this rate, it's gonna take forever to find any survivors. If there even are any."

The members of Corman Team looked to Corporal Sean Regal. He knew the unspoken question.

Is it even worth it to go further?

"Actually, I might have a solution for that," Howard said. He connected another cord from his tablet to the station's computer and began typing at an accelerated speed. A schematic of the station came up, with a small red highlight marked on North Section. "Bingo."

"The hell is that?" Laurie asked.

"As the corporal had mentioned, the place is on reserve power. Aside from here, it appears the station's main computer has shut down all unnecessary functions in order to keep the batteries alive as long as possible. Anything that is being used has to be activated manually or with an override." He put his finger to the highlighted area on the screen. "There's some power being used here. Minor stuff; lights, plumbing, and so forth. In simple terms: someone might be there."

Thomas took a closer look at the screen. "Can you get me an exact location?"

Howard worked his magic and brought up the coordinates. "Med/Lab, Room N-218."

Thomas turned to Sean. "Are we able to contact that room directly?"

"Yeah." Sean moved to an overly stuffed filing cabinet on the left end of the desk and pulled out a big book. "Each room should have a phone. Just give me a sec here..." He flipped through the pages until he reached the numbers of North Section. "Let's see here... Two-eighteen... ah-ha. Found it."

He picked up the desk's phone and dialed the number.

**

May Dyner found herself dozing in and out of a hazy half-dream. No matter how much she wanted to, her brain failed to commit to real sleep, especially not with Feinstein's snoring. That, and the lack of environmental stimulation from the station's automatic lighting system. Typically, the brightness in the corridor lights and those of the main workstations were designed to mimic the passing of a standard day. In the time they had been trapped in this little room, it grew extremely difficult to get any real rest. Plus, there was a situational awareness which kept the mind active. Then there was the fact there was only one narrow bed, and even that was not very comfortable.

She was leaning against the sink cabinet, trying to reminisce about life growing up in her home city. Her parents owned a typical two-story home. Nothing special. But when one became an adult, he or she grew to appreciate those things all the more. It was one of the reasons she worked for the company; to be able to afford her own two-story house with fifteen-hundred square feet of space. Maybe she would finally settle down and have a kid or two.

The peaceful thoughts were interrupted by intervals of dread, which came in flashes of black claws and grotesque hissing. They were mean-spirited reminders of her present reality and the unlikelihood of escaping it.

Even worse was the grating sound of Feinstein's snoring.

Without even opening her eyes, May felt around the floor in search of anything to chuck at the moron. She remembered he was near the restroom. Clearly, he had no issues sleeping.

Her hand found the edge of the cabinet and pulled it open. Inside was a bag of cotton balls. Eyes still closed, she hurled it over the bed. It hit the back wall and fell, landing right on the guy.

He woke up with a snort. "Wha--?"

"Serves you right," May groaned. "You're practically ringing the dinner bell with that noise."

She zoned off again...then stirred after an even more gravelly snore. Her blood pressure shot up. This could not be happening. Every other inconvenience of sleeping in this medical room she could deal with. But the snoring was just too much. And, clearly, nothing but a miracle was going to wake Feinstein up.

CHIRP-CHIRP-CHIRP-CHIRP-CHIRP!

It was a sound nobody expected to hear. For May, she thought she was in the midst of another dream. Sure, it was a dream of her being at work, but anything was better than trying to avoid flesh-eating monsters.

She sat up and flipped the lights on. Everyone, including Feinstein, was awake.

The miracle was real. The phone was ringing.

"Please tell me I'm not hearing things," Moses said.

"Nope!" May shot off the floor and rushed to the phone. She yanked it from its unit and put it to her ear. "Hello?"

"This is Corporal Sean Regal of Brom-Caylen Rapid Response Forces. To whom am I speaking?"

May pumped a fist, confirming to the others that help had arrived. The group made a silent cheer, barely containing a loud celebratory noise.

"This is May Dyner. Thank God you're here."

"How many are you?"

May felt her heart skip a beat. The line was breaking up quickly.

"Four of us. No severe injuries. Unfortunately, we're all that's left."

"Just the four of you?"

"Yes." Right then, it dawned on her—this guy was unaware of what they were facing. "Listen, Corporal, you need to be careful. This station, it's…" She heard the typical hum of a dead line. "Hello? Damn it."

She tried to return dial, but it failed to go through.

"It's alright," Alexandra said. "They know we're here! We're saved!"

May put the phone down. "I don't think they know what's out there." She thought about how easily the station's security guys were overpowered, even with the advantage of firearms on their side.

The room went silent.

Feinstein sank back to his spot, slowly taking in the facts. Rescue was no good if they were simply going to be added to the menu.

"Oh, God…"

***

"Damn it." Sean Regal attempted to redial, but the line was dead. "She was trying to tell me something, but it cut out. I can't get her back."

"Probably damage to the lines," Thomas said. "But at least we have confirmation that they're there."

"How many are there?" Charity asked.

"Four," Sean answered.

"Can't do much for them unless we can get out of here," Renee said.

"Shouldn't be a problem," Sean said. "You said it could be opened from the outside. Let me get the boss on the horn."

***

"Understood, sir."

It was the answer Durell expected to hear. As much as an investment the *Scarlett Caldera* was, the ramifications of the truth becoming public were far more drastic. Besides, as the boss had informed him, it had served its true purpose for the most part.

"I'll have my men set it up," he continued. "And what of Corman Team?... Yes, they're with the specialists from G.O.R.E. Sector... Alright, I just wanted to clear that up first... Copy that. Over and out."

He placed the headset down and turned to his left as Urich stepped out of the stairwell. Judging by the look on the operative's face, he knew precisely what was said during the private conversation.

"What's the status of the sweep?" Durell asked.

"South Section is secured. Place is empty. Whatever happened here, we missed it by a mile." Urich tilted his head at the desk's radio unit. "They really want to take it that far?"

"That's right," Durell said. "The order is given: November-Tango-Six."

Urich bit his lip. While he did not expect this trip to be a walk in the park, he certainly did not expect to be instructed to demolish the *Scarlett Caldera.*

"What of the others?"

Durell pierced his soul with a momentous stare. "The *Corman's* out of commission. Not enough room on the *Revere.* Only way for them to escape is through the G.O.R.E. submarine, and that would defeat the purpose, as they're the main reason we're imploding this place."

Urich looked away, visibly uncomfortable with the course of events. "Could Sean's team commandeer their sub? Take it by force?"

"You really think that thing doesn't have safeguards?" Durell said. "Not to mention the control system is probably way different. Bottom line; we don't have a lot of time, and I want to get this done as soon as possible."

It was in the middle of that statement when Sean Regal's voice came through the radio.

"Corman Team to Revere Team. You there, Durell?"

"Yeah, go ahead."

"Sir, we have a line on some survivors. They're in North Section. As far as we know, they're the only ones left in the whole station."

"Copy that," Durell said. "Is West Section secure?"

"Negative. That was the other thing. The processing station over here has been locked down. We cannot get out unless you guys manage to do some kind of override."

Durell cracked a diabolical smile. This call could not have come at a better time.

"Copy that, Corporal. I'll get right on it. In fact, I think I'll be able to clear a path for you; that way we shouldn't face any obstacles on our way there. Give me one sec."

"Sounds good, sir."

Durell put himself back on the computer, and pulled out his own smartphone to look up specific access codes.

Urich stood over him, quickly reading his body language. Durell typed in the access codes, then instructed the computer to open every passageway inside the entire station.

A series of shifting gears vibrated through the facility as every pressurized door opened.

"Door's open! Much appreciated, boss. We're heading to North Section."

"Copy that. Be careful. We'll be right there with you."

As Durell lied, he typed in another code. Right then, the system froze up. Precisely as intended.

Urich knew the plan. "Not even the automated emergency systems can shut the place down. You just turned the place into a death trap. One small breach can implode the entire station."

Durell grinned at his subordinate's ability to feign contempt. While Urich may have felt some mild concern for the well-being of Corman Team, he ultimately knew what he had signed on for. At the end of the day, his paycheck was what really mattered. Better yet, given the severity of what they were instructed to do, the "Old Man" would probably give them a hell of a bonus just to put their minds at ease.

"This way, all we have to do is plant charges in South Section. Tell the guys to start planting charges on the south wall. Particularly near any portholes and airlocks they can find. And don't use the main frequency."

CHAPTER 11

Howard brought up the schematic of the entire complex and isolated the most direct route to Med/Lab.

"Should only take you a couple of minutes to get there if you move quickly."

"Good." Thomas moved to the door and motioned at Archer to take point. "Howard, stay here and guide us through the comms, and guard the sub. Renee? You good with keeping him company?"

The lieutenant's face was contorted as she peered into the eerie darkness beyond the open doorway.

"Absolutely."

Thomas looked to Sean. "Careful with those rifles."

"We've got suppressors," the merc with the silver hair, Spencer, remarked. "They're the good ones too. You won't have to worry about your ears."

"I'm not so much worried about the sound as much as I am you not watching your background," Thomas responded. "Guns and pressurized facilities don't mix. That's why we're taking point."

All of Corman Team looked to their corporal. Every one of their faces conveyed the same question.

You going to take a backseat to this guy?

Sean had no qualms with the idea. Out of the whole group, he was the only one with the sense to be grateful for Raptor Pack's intervention with the sharks.

"Whatever Captain Rodney says, we'll comply," he informed them. His teammates managed to keep a straight face, though Thomas could sense the reluctance and bitterness.

He imagined the corporation must have been paying a nice wage to earn this degree of loyalty.

"Archer, lead the way."

The sniper activated a flashlight on the barrel of his gun then moved into the stairwell. Thomas and Renee were behind him, watching the walls in addition to the steps. Sean and his men followed, keeping five feet of distance from each other as they ascended to the next deck.

They arrived on B Deck of West Section. Offices and lounge areas were cloaked in darkness and a stale, metal odor. Pipes dripped from overhead in a steady beat, each droplet exploding into a dozen tinier ones after connecting with the tile floor.

Archer was thorough in his sweep. While this area was not the objective, he wanted to make sure they would not have to face any surprises on their return trip. So far, they found nothing but the aftermath of the station's downfall. Tables were broken in pieces, food was scattered about, utensils—particularly knives—lay all over the floor, most of them near blood stains.

Markings, similar to those in the processing room, lined the walls, floor, and furniture. The pantry and refrigerator had been torn open by force and their contents ripped to shreds.

Whatever had come through here, it had a hell of an appetite, and it wasn't biased on whether its meal was raw meat or processed canned goods.

Howard's voice came through the comm. *"If you go back to the north corridor, you'll find the tunnel entrance forty paces to the west."*

Thomas took point this time, aiming his rifle and light down the grey passageway. He saw more dripping pipes, battered tiles, and an open entryway connecting West Section to North.

"Check. Got it."

They closed in on the destination, then came to a sudden stop after noticing an open air duct past the tunnel. There, a thousand markings stretched in all directions like lines on a map.

Thomas leaned over to Charity, who was staring with a sentiment of trepidation that was plain on her face.

"Something come to mind?" he whispered.

She nodded. "Whatever these things are, they're working in unison. They might be able to plan coordinated attacks."

"Did she say what I think she said?" Spencer whispered.

"Shh!" Duke hissed.

"Don't 'shh' me," Spencer replied. "I'm not keen on walking into a trap."

"No, we're going forward," Sean replied. "I don't want to hear any more arguments."

Thomas ignored the chatter behind him and continued consulting with the biologist. "You think they've figured out the layout of this place?"

"It's possible," she said. "They obviously figured out how to use the air ducts to escape the processing area. They've got to be holed up somewhere. Probably gorging on food in another galley or lounge area elsewhere in the station."

Thomas nodded. "The opening of the doors might've just rung the dinner bell." He shouldered his weapon. By now, he was committed to the objective. "Let's hope we've got enough firepower to even the odds."

After receiving the hand motion from his captain, Ray Archer moved into the tunnel. With caution, he led the way into North Section.

***

"Can you reach them?"

May Dyner brought the phone over her shoulder and took a breath, managing to prevent herself from smashing it against the wall in frustration. It was the faulty wiring and the repeated questioning by Moses that got her blood boiling.

Exhaling slowly, she managed to give an answer while mostly appearing stable. "If I did, you'd probably know by the lively conversation I'd be having with the guy on the other end of the line."

Moses made a 'hmm' sound, then shrugged. "Good point."

May looked over at Alexandra. She was sitting on the patient bed, arms wrapped around her knees, both enlightened at the knowledge of a rescue attempt and anxious of what awaited them.

"You alright?" May asked.

Alexandra shook her head. "I like my job, May. But I don't want to be eaten."

"I know."

"Do you think they'll be able to kill all of those things and get this station back up and running?"

May scoffed. It was a state of mind she could not relate to. Here Alexandra sat, barely keeping herself mentally stable, and yet her primary concern was coming back to the bowls of the Pacific in hopes of resuming her job? Not many people had a mind to return to a place of such horror, especially while still actively trapped in a predicament they might not get out of.

"There's other jobs, you know?"

Alexandra shook her head. "Not for me. You know this."

May sighed. The company had firmly snared her with its financial tendrils. They were good like that.

She looked over at Feinstein. He was up on the countertop, ear to the vent.

"What's the matter?" she asked. "You hear more movement?"

Hearing herself say that out loud, she grabbed a small scalpel from one of the drawers and readied herself for an intrusion.

Feinstein nodded, but did not share her call to action.

"A bunch of them are moving *away*. A lot of them, by the sound of it." He paused and listened for a few more moments. "There's still a couple out there. They know we're here. They just can't get in."

"But the rest have left?" Moses said. "Does it have anything to do with that sound we heard?"

"The doors opening up?" Feinstein said. "Probably. I think those guys cleared themselves a path. In doing so, those things are free to roam around. Considering how fast they went, they've got wind of some fresh meat."

Moses swallowed. "Doesn't bode well for our new friends."

"Christ." May frantically tapped on the phone buttons, praying this time she would be able to connect with the processing station.

Meanwhile, Alexandra resumed hugging her knees. It proved to be as productive as May's attempts to make a phone call.

***

"Once you enter North Section, you'll want to cut through Med Bay office areas," Howard said.

The team entered North Section and beheld several fallen ceiling tiles, ravaged cubical barriers, and an eerie silence that was occasionally interrupted by a faint shift in air currents. Every so often, they would hear the station groan from the pressure outside, and the automated mechanics that kept the *Scarlett Caldera* functioning hummed and whirred.

They were in the main medical station. Right off the bat, they found two hospital beds that had been flayed open. On the floor were shreds of the mattress, hospital gowns, and all sorts of emergency surgical equipment that was being put to use before everything went dark.

Like with everywhere else the group had inspected, there were no bodies. Just blood and several quiet rooms left in a battered state.

It further enhanced the mental image of what had occurred. The overrunning of the station did not happen in minutes. It took a little bit of time; enough for some injured workers to be attended to. That was not to say it was not fast. Clearly, the emergency procedures that were underway were unable to be completed.

Other rooms of Med/Lab had their doors torn off the hinges. Everywhere the flashlights swept, there were markings caused by razor-sharp appendages. CO_2 fire extinguishers lay about, their contents staining the tile floor after having been deployed. Chairs, meter sticks, and even cabinet drawers lay in a mess, all of which were nowhere near their original destination.

Thomas put himself in the shoes of a frightened worker trying to back away from some sort of multi-limbed organism with a lust for bloodshed. He imagined himself grabbing ahold of whatever he could and chucking it at the attacker, only for the beast to keep on coming without a care or concern in the world.

"Hold position," he said. He looked over at Sean. "Where's the other team?"

Sean cupped his mic so he could whisper into it. "Corman Team to Revere? What's your twenty?"

"We're cutting through the East Section," Durell said. *"We're moving with haste. We'll be in North Section in approximately three minutes."*

Sean lowered his mic and looked at Thomas. "He says three minutes."

"Three minutes?" Thomas' eyebrows shot to his hairline. "The hell's taking them so long?"

"He says they're in East Section," Sean said.

Thomas tilted his head, glancing at Charity and Archer as he tried to make sense of what he just heard.

"East Section? Why would he cut through there if he opened up a path from West?"

Sean swallowed. As he thought about it, he too realized it did not make much sense; and Durell was not the kind of guy who did random things. Every decision he made had a purpose, even something as seemingly simple as going left or right.

"Should we wait?" he asked the captain.

"Negative," Thomas said. "Let's wrap this up and get back to the *McQueen*."

Archer listened to Howard's instructions and followed a path through Med/Lab.

Here, there were more than just medical pods. There were advanced research laboratories, with all sorts of advanced equipment made for analyzing things on a microscopic level. Gene-sequencing computers sat quietly on desks comprised of thick steel with plastic layering. A few green lights twinkled as the reserve power kept the machines alive and available for use.

Charity moved over to one of them and took a seat.

Thomas stopped. "What are you doing, Doctor?"

"I want to see what they were up to. Clearly, these computers were designed to stay functional even in the event of a major emergency."

She wiggled the mouse. Fortunately, no password was needed to wake the computer up. Being three miles under the surface, the researchers here were not concerned with unauthorized personnel getting a glance at what they were up to.

A series of images and codes appeared on the screen. To Thomas Rodney, it was a bunch of gibberish. For Charity, it was like looking at the recipe for Armageddon.

"What is it?" Thomas asked.

"The bastards," she hissed. "They knew exactly what they were doing. This facility was never meant for developing renewable energy. That was the big selling point to give to the public. Not only were they looking for the meteorite, but they were exposing the mineral to test subjects."

"Test subjects?" Thomas said. "What kind of test subjects?"

Charity began combing through the computer for other files.

At this point, the security officer named Duke stepped in. "What the hell is this? Corporal, are you gonna allow this? She's going through company files! These are confidential."

Sean did nothing to stop her. If anything, he was as curious as Raptor Pack as to what the company was working on. He knew about the meteorite, but as far as experiments went, he was uncertain.

Charity clicked a few icons on the screen.

Various images popped up; profiles of all sorts of deep-sea life, known and newly discovered.

Starfish; anglerfish, crustaceans, a type of newly discovered shark, worms, squids, and many more.

She pulled up a video file.

In the little digital box was footage of several scientists working in this very lab. One of then had a syringe loaded with a purple fluid. Strapped to an operating table was a large fish with a transparent body. It had a pipe hooked up to its mouth to keep water flowing over its gills.

The scientist with the needle slowly worked it into the flesh, then emptied the syringe.

"They're injecting the mineral directly into the bloodstream," Charity said.

The change was immediate. The poor fish began convulsing. Bulges took form all over its body. Its color went through all sorts of changes. Its skeletal structure appeared to shift, as the fish bent out of proportion and increased in size.

"You once told me only a particle was needed to mutate something," Thomas said. "That looks like they were giving it a heavy dose."

"You'd be correct," Charity said. "Normally, the mutation happens over a period of time. Sometimes months. Sometimes years. But the quantity they're giving is obviously causing rapid mutation."

"Not just rapid," Thomas said, watching the progression of events on the screen.

By now, the scientists were in a panic, having regretted the dosage. The fish was more than twice as long as it originally was. Its jaws had enhanced, its teeth growing at the same rate as the rest of its body. It bit through the pump and lifted its head off the table to snap at one of the workers.

One of the security personnel ran into frame and stuck a shotgun in the animal's mouth.

Boom!

The fish went limp, the back of its head opened up and smoking. It was at this point where the video ended.

Charity stood up, her face noticeably red even in the dim lighting from the screen. "Those idiots don't realize what they're messing with."

"You think they created those sharks out there?" Thomas asked.

"No," she answered. "I think those were exposed to the meteorite itself. Them, and the things that infested this place. Based on what we've seen, it's obvious they weren't deliberately mutated. That said, we can only imagine what else the company was doing with the mineral."

Thomas turned his eyes to Sean and the men under his lead. The corporal looked as though he might be sick, his eyes still glued to the screen despite the video having concluded.

"You mean to tell me you're shocked by this?" Thomas said to him. "You knew they were harvesting the mineral. What did you think they were planning to do with it? Make bigger children's playsets?"

Sean shook his head. "It's as simple as this: before, I was able to turn a blind eye to everything and believe the propaganda. As long as my check cleared and I was *told* that nothing illicit would come as a result of the project. But now, I've seen it with my own eyes. Brom-Caylen opened Pandora's Box, and they might not be able to shut it."

"Captain?" Howard said in a very concerned tone.

"Yes, Doctor?"

"I think there's something coming up on you. I was able to tap into some of the security cameras between you and Room 218, and I thought I saw something. Movement. Coming in from the north. Corridor B-3... uh, that's one o'clock to your current position."

The security team moved forward, passing by the Raptor Pack personnel in an attempt to take charge.

"Pull back," Thomas hissed. "We don't know what—"

An echo swept through the room. It was a metallic tearing sound, as though a giant can opener was being taken to one of the bulkheads.

All nine members of the group froze in place. Brian and Laurie stood at the upper left corner of the room, keeping their weapons pointed up ahead at the north door. Spencer and Omar waited by a doorway on the righthand side, where this lab connected to another one. Duke watched the rear, hoping to catch a glance of Revere Team, should they approach.

Sean stood close to Raptor Pack, his rifle pointed straight ahead.

A minute passed.

Silence encompassed the group.

During that time, nobody moved. Not a single sound was heard, whether it be in the lab, or elsewhere.

"Switch to thermal vision," Sean whispered.

Charity raised a hand. "Most animals down here are not warm-blooded. You won't spot them using that tech."

Her warning went unheard by the rest of the security team. Goggles were placed over their eyes, and a few moments later, they were carefully combing through the entire lab.

Brian moved to the doorway. His finger slipped into the trigger guard and hugged the slanted piece of metal inside. He exited the lab and pointed his gun to the right in the direction of the recent sound.

He held position for several seconds before Laurie joined him in the intersecting corridor. He peeked down the corridor, then ducked back into the lab room.

"You see something?" Charity asked.

"A whole section of the ceiling is hanging free," Brian whispered. "It's like something came down through the ducts."

Thomas felt his blood run cold.

Or they tore it down and went UP.

A burst of sound made the entire group turn on their heels. Several parts of the overhead fell free, landing all around a flabbergasted Duke.

The soldier pointed his weapon skyward, then gasped in utter shock as he was embraced by a mass of rigid claws and spindly legs.

Through the breach came an organism shaped like an ordinary millipede, with arms of a praying mantis protruding from its upper body. Its head was considerably wider than the rest of its jet-black body, and armed with a corkscrew array of razor-sharp mandibles.

Dozens of legs fidgeted on both sides of its eight-foot body, all serving equal parts weapon and means of transportation.

It descended on Duke, its forelegs acting like katanas in their killing efficiency.

The soldier went down, his rifle spitting rounds uselessly into the overhead. Mandibles and forelegs tore through his Kevlar and into his flesh, producing thick eruptions of blood.

"Holy dear God!" Sean exclaimed.

Thomas, Charity, and Archer did not allow themselves to be distracted by the awe of such an organism. They shouldered their weapons and put them to the test.

Bright blue streaks of blazing-hot energy zipped from their muzzles and connected with the crustacean's rigid exoskeleton. The armored shell managed to absorb the first few rounds, transferring enough pain signals to the mutant's brain to get it to face the challengers head-on. More energy bolts managed to cut through its defenses, turning its black shell orange and grey. Soon, blue-green guts spilled from the charred gorges.

The crustacean let out a shallow, yet simultaneously high-pitched hiss that pierced the hearts of every man in the room.

Thomas quickly tired of the sound and planted a blazing bolt of energy in the center of its mandibles. Mouthparts spat out with strings of green blood. More hits to the creature's face deepened the crater, and in a few moments, its head was reduced to a simmering pile of flesh atop an elongated body.

Its corpse slumped over that of Duke's, its blood mixing with his.

Sean rushed to the soldier's side and checked his pulse, then stood up and shook his head, confirming the obvious.

"Holy crap," Spencer exclaimed.

"We got it," Omar said with triumph, seemingly overlooking the fact that one of their own was KIA. "Nice work, monster hunters. Those guns, where can I get me one of—"

The ceiling above him split apart. From the center came another crustacean, its bulging eyes reflecting his flashlight. In that glow were twirling mandibles and thrashing legs, all of which were aiming to carve through flesh and bone.

Omar was knocked to the floor. Right away, he hollered in agony as those instruments of death began cutting through him.

A panicked Spencer put his rifle muzzle to the creature's head and pulled the trigger. The round ricocheted off his exoskeleton and struck his shin, dropping the ornery soldier to the floor.

The other took aim, but could not get a clear shot with Omar directly under the coiling body.

Forelegs and spiky limbs dug into the soldier's body, effortlessly cutting through his vest and the soft meat under it.

For the second time in a row, Raptor Pack intervened with their plasma rifles. Blazing hot bolts of energy struck the centipede crustacean, lifting its head off the dying Omar as pain surged through its body.

Archer planted a few rounds on its head, blasting off its pair of antennae. The loss of its sensory organs put the creature in a frenzy. It rolled off Omar, twisting itself into a pretzel shape.

Raptor Pack continued the punishment, their deadly projectiles burning through the exoskeleton and savaging the soft organs inside.

The hissing ceased and the legs stiffened. A smell of charred flesh filled the laboratory. The creature was dead.

Right away, Archer moved for the north door.

Thomas did not bother to question what was on his mind. Instead, he and Charity were right behind him.

They went into the passageway and took a right, then hooked left at the juncture where the creatures had torn into the ceiling. Archer unclipped something from his vest and held it up to his teammates, simultaneously telling them what was on his mind and warning them to turn away.

In his hand was a flash grenade.

Thomas pulled up a janitor's cart, then turned away.

Archer tossed the thing into the breach, then shielded his eyes. Even through the protection of their eyelids and hands, they saw the blistering flash. More importantly, they heard the hisses of other creatures that were waiting up there.

Archer stepped onto the cart and aimed his light into the ceiling, where two of the creatures squirmed in agony. He worsened their misery with a barrage of blaster bolts, concentrating on headshots to make his kills as quick and efficient as possible.

In the end, the pair of deep-sea crustaceans lay dead, their combined weight weighing on the overhead panels.

"Good call," Thomas said.

Archer stepped down and replaced his battery mag.

Sean and his three surviving team members joined them. Brian and Laurie assisted the injured Spencer, who hopped on his one good leg.

"To hell with this," Spencer said. "I say we get the hell out of here!"

"What the hell are those things?!" Laurie said.

All eyes turned to Charity.

"Some kind of crustacean," she explained. "I don't know what it mutated from. I'm inclined to believe it is a previously undiscovered organism, unearthed during the excavation. They were exposed to the meteorite and must've been burrowed into the rock sample that was brought into the processing station. Once there, they awakened and went on a killing spree."

"Wait," Sean said. "You think they were just 'sleeping' in that chunk of rock?"

"It's the only thing that makes sense," Charity said. She immediately put her hand over her mouth. "Well, one of two things…"

"I knew it," Brian muttered.

"Either they were burrowed in there… or there were eggs, which then hatched once the sample was brought inside," she said.

"Wait…" Spencer made a sound that was half-laugh, half-whimper. "If those things hatched from eggs, would that mean a big one… I mean, a *really* big one, laid them?"

Charity bit her lip. "That would stand to reason."

Spencer hung his head down. "I need a drink."

Thomas reloaded his weapon and joined Archer as he began to move up the next passageway.

"The next section of Med/Lab is up here," he said. "Let's get these people, and we'll be on our merry way."

The remainder of Corman Team responded well to that statement.

Brian tapped Spencer on the back. "The faster we do this, the faster you get that drink."

"As long as I freaking get it," Spencer said.

They moved north, checking the number on each medical room. For a site with relatively few people, they had enough rooms and equipment to provide care for a small town. It was enough for Thomas to suspect the company was thinking of adding more personnel down here. Considering what the true purpose of the *Scarlett Caldera* was, it made sense they would need as much medical supplies as possible.

They arrived at room N-218.

The door was barricaded. Furthermore, it was welded shut, evidenced by the blending of metal at the frame.

Thomas banged his fist on the door. "This is G.O.R.E. Sector, working with Brom-Caylen Security! If anyone is in there, please respond."

He heard a knock in response.

"Yes!" a female voice called out. "Give us a sec! We'll get this thing opened up."

"Don't worry. We'll handle it. Get away from the door." Thomas looked to Archer. A true professional who required little instruction, the guy was already in the process of preparing a charge. He placed it on the door, armed it, then moved to the other side of the hall.

A small explosion separated the door from the welding as well as its hinges.

Thomas kicked it open and stepped into a joint set of rooms. In the one on the left were four survivors; two men and two women.

One of those women, a redhead with a fit build and a look of utmost relief on her face, stepped forward.

"Thank God!"

"I like to think He's on our side," Thomas said. "Are any of you hurt? Any immediate medical attention needed?"

"Thankfully, no," she said. "My name's May Dyner. Behind me is Alexadra, Moses, and Feinstein. We honestly don't even know how long we've been stuck in here."

"Too long," the big man named Feinstein exclaimed.

"Can't begrudge you that feeling," Charity said.

"Thank God you made it," Alexandra said. "We wanted to warn you of those things, but the damn phone line must've been damaged at some point."

"Yeah," Moses said. "We were certain you would not be able to get past all of those things. But hey, I guess you monster hunters are even better than we thought!"

Charity smiled and shrugged confidently. "What can we say? Takes more than a handful of underwater crustaceans to stop us."

What was meant to be an uplifting statement only caused the survivors to sour. May's smile shrank, then turned into a full frown after she took the liberty of peeking into the passageway.

"Something the matter?" Sean asked.

"A handful?" May asked.

"Mind if we ask how many you consider to be a handful?" Feinstein asked with a nervous smile on his face. "Please say twenty-to-thirty."

At this point, even Archer was looking uneasy.

"Um, no," Charity said. "More like… four."

The group of survivors exchanged confused glances.

"You mean to say there's more?" Sean asked.

"A lot more," May said. "We could hear them through the vents. They knew we were in here, but there was no decent way in. There's no space in the overhead above this room, and the vents are too small. But they were not keen on giving up, so they just hung out, probably hoping we'd wander out."

"We heard them move off," Feinstein said. "We thought they were going to intercept you guys. I guess a few stayed behind."

"But the rest..." Moses shrugged. "They could be anywhere."

Sean Regal was glancing anxiously at the overhead and the depths of the passageway.

"You said twenty-to-thirty?"

"That's right," May replied.

Now, Charity mirrored the Corporal's body language. Every shadow was full of menace. Her eyes were quick to start playing tricks on her. Every texture of the walls and overhead suddenly resembled a hungry crustacean, eager to dig into her flesh.

"If they aren't here, where are they now?"

CHAPTER 12

"Revere Team, this is Corporal Regal from Corman. We've located the survivors and are on our way back to the West Section processing station. What's your location?"

Durell ground his teeth as he placed the last explosive on C Deck of South Section. "Um, sorry. We got held up on the west side. Had, uh, some barricades that must've been made by the crew. Not sure what they were defending against, but they were good at blocking our paths."

"Copy that. On that note, sir, we've made contact with the threat. Big... bug things. The doctor lady refers to them as crustaceans, though they don't look like any crab or lobster I've ever seen. That said, they're vicious. Omar and Duke are KIA, and Spencer is injured. Might take us a little longer to get back."

Durell armed the explosive and began moving to the nearest stairwell, all while reminding himself to feign compassion for the deceased personnel.

"Damn it. Okay, well done, Corporal. Take your time heading back. Watch your surroundings. We're heading back to the *Revere.*"

"Copy."

He sensed a hint of confusion in Sean's voice. Never was Durell ever compassionate, even when presented with the fatalities of his men. His reputation preceded him, and in most cases that was a plus. But when lying, it worked against him.

Not that it mattered. In two minutes, Sean and those Raptor Pack bastards would be nobody's problem... all

99

due to the 'accident' that caused the catastrophic implosion of the *Scarlett Caldera*.

He switched to the second frequency. "Urich, is everyone assembled by the *Revere?*"

"I'm here with Gates and Roland. Waiting on everyone else."

"Wynorski here. I'm heading down from B Deck with Hiram."

"This is Petri. I'm finishing up on A Deck. About to join you guys."

"Well, hurry up," Durrell said. "If you heard the chatter between myself and Regal, then you know what's up."

Taking his own advice, he moved to the stairwell and descended to the processing station. Boots pounded the steps above him as Wynorski and Hiram rushed downstairs, eager to get to the sub before their boss got in too much of a hurry.

They arrived in the processing station, where Urich, Roland, and Gates were waiting.

"Everyone ready to board?" Urich said.

"Only if you have the timer set," Durell replied.

Urich held up a device. "You know, we can just blow the charges with this."

"Yeah. *If* the signal can get through the big steel walls," Durell said. "Set the timer. If we can't blow the charges, we can at least disable the lift for West Section to keep the other group from leaving before they go off."

"Hope you're right," Urich said. "Because this thing is set for thirty minutes."

"Good." Durell looked over his shoulder. "Where the hell is Petri?"

Urich used the secondary comm. "Petri? What's the holdup?"

No answer came through.

Durell stomped his boot onto the deck. "I'm gonna kill that moron." He looked at the hatch where the sub was connected, then at the detonator in Urich's hand. "Maybe literally."

"Just give him a minute, please," Roland said. "He's up on A Deck. It's just taking him an extra minute."

Thump! Thump! Thump!

Roland looked to the vibrations coming from the stairwell. "See? He's almost here. Just took him a little long—" He looked to the east wall. Several vibrations were passing through the ducts. They were subtle at first, easily mistaken for air passing through. Now, it was as though a full hurricane was tearing through the veins of the station, as well as the stairwell.

The overhead rattled, as did the west wall.

Urich backed up to the hatch. "What the…"

As though propelled by an air compressor, the opening to one of the ducts popped off the wall. From the opening came a creature that was familiar, yet totally alien in its physicality. Eight feet in length, carried by over thirty legs on each side of its body, and equipped with two forelegs shaped like curved swords, it darted across the wall.

Another one appeared in its place. Then another.

A piece of tile fell from the overhead, making way for a fourth centipede creature. A fifth appeared, then a sixth.

A seventh and eighth came in from the east wall, while a ninth and tenth emerged from the stairwell.

"What in the name of—" Roland started blasting away.

One of the creatures sprang off the east wall and tackled him to the floor. Forelegs, lined with wedge-shaped spurs, sliced through his gear and into his flesh, sparking a world of pain and an ocean of blood.

Another one dropped from the overhead on top of Gates. Bullets zipped aimlessly from his rifle as the soldier was overpowered. A slice of one of those forelegs severed his hand, which dropped from his wrist, still squeezing the trigger.

The weapon hit the deck, still spitting bullets. One of them punched a hole through Urich's left foot, dropping the ex-marine. Squealing in pain and fear, he scampered to the hatch.

Durell attempted to move after him, but only made two steps before one of those things sprang in his direction.

Legs thrashed and those multi-jointed arms extended. One of them nicked his upper left arm, slicing the sleeve and lacerating the skin.

"Holy..." He jumped back, momentarily overcome with a rare feeling of absolute terror. The beast landed in a half-coiled pose a few feet in front of him. It rose on its bottom half like a rattlesnake, its body bending at countless segments attached to one another by sheets of thin, flexible material to allow freedom of movement. The legs quivered, on the verge of delivering the freak of nature to its next kill.

Durell put his rifle muzzle to its face and squeezed the trigger. The bug-thing reeled backward, its shell scarred by the point-blank impact. He continued shooting the thing, gradually feeling alarmed at the lack of significant damage inflicted by his weapon.

The creature coiled on the floor, sprawling on all of its many legs.

Seeing that it was about to scurry, Durell went on the offensive. He put his rifle muzzle to one of those big black eyes and fired again. Unlike the exoskeleton, the eye proved no match for the full-metal jackets inside his magazine. Green fluid spewed from its face as it writhed on the deck, slowly succumbing to its death.

Durell looked over his right shoulder to the sound of screams.

Gates was kicking his feet and paddling his arms in the air, the rest of him completely obscured by two crustaceans that happily flayed him open from top to bottom.

Several yards beyond him was Wynorski. He attempted to retreat to the stairwell, wailing as one of the creatures clamped its mandibles over his left ankle. He fired his last few rounds against its forehead, failing to penetrate the shell. His final shot deflected off the creature's forehead and struck his other leg, dropping him.

"Oh, God!"

He drew his sidearm and proceeded to fire into the swarm as they gathered around him. The meager defense proved even more insufficient, doing little more than delaying the creatures by a few milliseconds.

They were all over him and commenced to digging in. The one clinging to his ankle pulled away, taking his foot with it. Others sliced with their forelegs, reforming Wynorski's body.

"Hey! Hey! HEY!"

Durell turned to the south, just in time to witness Urich slam the hatch door shut. The wheel turned, sealing it completely. A green light flashed, signaling that the station was ready for the *Revere* to detach.

Banging on that door was Hirum, who was moments away from joining Urich in his retreat.

"Urich! You bastard!"

A long and narrow shadow with many quivering digits on each side encompassed him. Hiram turned around, dropped his weapon, threw his arms over his eyes like a child, and screamed.

The crustacean lunged, pinning him against the wall while sinking its jaws into his jugular.

Behind the gushing of blood and the gurgling sounds that started as screams came a deep *THUD* from the *Revere* detaching.

Durell could not believe his situation. In thirty seconds, his team was wiped out and his ride was stolen. If there was anything working in his favor, it was that most of the creatures were preoccupied with feasting on his teammates, granting him an opportunity to escape.

Weaving around the horde, Durell sprinted for the stairwell. As he did, more creatures emerged from the walls and joined the feeding frenzy. And 'frenzy' was the word, with jet-black millipede-shaped organisms slashing at one another for possession of the corpses.

Naturally, some of those new arrivals took notice of the one survivor.

Durell sprinted up the steps, then paused after hearing more screeching sounds above him. Drops of blood and slime rained through the twisting rows of stairs.

With more of those things emerging below him, Durell had no choice but to ascend.

He reached the C Deck tunnel entrance and took another look at the mayhem taking place above him. On the platform near B Deck's entrance, three crustaceans enjoyed peeling Petri apart. Of course, there was little at this point to identify Petri—Durell only knew it was him thanks to the process of elimination.

He entered the northwest tunnel and made a sprint for West Section.

***

Urich's foot was pulsing. Eight years in the Marine Corps, six years as a private contractor, and never once had he actually absorbed a bullet. On two other occasions, he had taken one in the vest, but today was the first time in his career one broke the skin. Even worse, it was his own damn bullet.

Feeling his own blood filling his boot, he reversed the *Revere* from the *Scarlett Caldera*. At this point, he considered his entire team to be KIA.

Clipped to his belt was the detonator. He had another two minutes to detonate the charges before the automatic timer began its countdown. First, he needed to make some distance from the facility. Being in close proximity to the implosion of a facility this large would be as devastating as standing next to a GBU-43/B Massive Ordinance Air Blast explosive.

He initiated ascent, watching the facility disappear into the darkness. As the sub lifted, he switched on the interior lights to inspect his foot.

Urich was no stranger to the sight of blood and mangled flesh, but it was always that of other people. Seeing his own set off an alarm in his head like nothing he had ever experienced before.

WHOOSH!

The *Revere* shuddered and turned to starboard, caught in a sudden current of ocean.

Urich sat up and looked out the window, catching a faint shadow rushing past the sub.

WHOOSH!

The *Revere* shook once more, now rotating slightly to port.

Urich clung to a handle above his seat, keeping himself stable through the turbulence. As the anomaly made its pass, he caught a fleeting glimpse of a half-moon-shaped fin at its rear.

The big shark.

His foot pulsed with increased intensity, fueled by an added surge of adrenaline and anxiety. In switching on the interior lights to inspect his injury, he essentially put a bullseye on himself.

He reached for a switch to turn the lights off.

By now, it did not matter.

Another current of water struck the *Revere*, displaced by the direct advance of the mutant shark as it moved in for the kill.

Urich managed to get a glimpse of its teeth… as they breached the cockpit.

***

BOOM!

A violent tremor shook the *Scarlett Caldera,* bringing the group to a halt. Thomas turned his eyes to the ceiling, watching the imperfections of the corridor jitter.

"That was not a pressure adjustment," he muttered. "That sounded like a blast…"

"Or an implosion," May Dyner said.

Thomas was inclined to agree. Something within him suspected the company employee had heard one or two similar events during her time down here.

"But from what?" Charity asked. "Did the company send another team down here? It definitely came from the outside. The only other group aside from us is… Durell's team."

All eyes turned to Sean.

Sharing their concern, he got on the horn with the boss. "Corman Team to Revere Team. What's your status?"

It was a few moments before a response transmission came through. Before any words were said, the group heard the sound of running footsteps and heavy breathing.

"We're overrun!" Durell said. *"I'm heading to West Section. I've got a bunch of freaks on my tail."*

"Copy that. We're on our way," Sean replied.

They were nearing the north entrance of West Section. Thomas looked around for a sense of where he needed to go to intercept Durell.

As though reading his mind, Howard's voice came through the radio.

"Captain, stay on the same level. Take a left turn, follow the hallway through the entire bend. You've got a little over a hundred meters to sprint before you arrive at the personnel tunnel to South Section."

"Copy. Thank you, Doctor."

"If those things get wind of our location, they'll swarm the *McQueen*," Charity said.

"Good thing we brought the right toys," Thomas said. "Right, Archer?"

True to his usual self, the sniper led the charge.

They followed the route provided by their trusty engineer, with Sean Regal running alongside them. Brian and Laurie remained with Spencer and continued to lead him to the processing station.

Running footsteps reverberated throughout the perimeter passageway. After two hundred paces, they heard additional steps coming from up ahead.

Lights beamed forward at a nearby juncture.

A running shadow took form, dwarfing its source. Durell emerged into the corridor and turned to face the source of light.

Sprinting at the team, he pointed his thumb over his shoulder and shouted, "They're coming!"

Sure enough, they were.

Four crustaceans emerged, two on the deck, the other two scurrying over the walls, leaving new markings with each rotating motion of their legs. They made a righthand turn to pursue their victim, then recoiled as the blinding lights scalded their eyes.

Once Durell was out of the line of fire, Raptor Pack opened fire. Multiple plasma bolts zipped from their guns right at the crustaceans. There was no reaction by the creatures; no cry of pain, nor was there a smell of charred flesh. The projectiles disappeared into a puff of hot smoke a few yards short of the creatures, as though an invisible barrier protected them.

Thomas squeezed his eyes shut. "Crap!"

Archer was cursing under his breath as well. Even he had forgotten about the one drawback of these weapons.

The crustaceans, no longer deterred by the blinding light, rushed the team, unwittingly putting themselves in range.

Thomas and Charity focused their fire on one of the creatures on the walls. Legs popped off, as did an antenna after a headshot. It took several hits before its exoskeleton deteriorated under the searing touch of the projectiles. Spilling green blood and spaghetti-like guts, it fell.

Archer focused a barrage of headshots on one of the creatures moving over the floor. Even with half its face blown off, the thing kept coming. It took the other half of its face being blown off to finally get the job done.

The group was forced to backpedal as the remaining two beasts closed in. Archer unleashed a few more shots, popping off several legs from the other crustacean climbing over the wall. It lost its grip and collapsed, landing near its brethren.

It twisted into all sorts of shapes like a worm being placed on a hook before righting itself.

The fourth one gradually closed the distance.

Durell, cursing every word in the book, loaded a fresh magazine and sprayed at the ugly thing.

Several of his rounds zipped over the creature's head and struck the wall on the lefthand side, ricochetting upward through the overhead.

A rapid hissing sound filled the corridor.

"Oh, hell!" Thomas said. He and Archer moved in opposite directions, right as the crustacean made a bounding leap. It passed in-between them, landing face-first just a few feet from Sean Regal.

With the wall directly behind him and the beast right in front, the corporal moved quickly with a desperate tactic. He shoved his rifle muzzle against the comparatively soft chitin between two of the body segments, then popped off several rounds.

The crustacean lurched away from him, bashing its head into the opposite wall. Its rear end swung like a baseball bat, sweeping Charity's feet out from under her.

Yelping, she landed on her back.

The beast lifted its head and turned to look at her. Jaws twisted into a bizarre contortion, wiry appendages frolicking over a honeycomb of deadly teeth.

She sat up and shoved her gun forward. "Nope!"

A single blast of burning plasma served as the last thing the beast would ever taste. It bent backward into a horseshoe shape, its head smoking and dripping fluid.

While it succumbed to its injury, the fourth member of its group returned to the wall and resumed an assault.

Archer and Thomas combined their firepower and hit the thing with a volley, centering their shots on the chitin. The centipede-like mutant dropped to the floor for the second time, now in four pieces.

Thomas lowered his weapon and turned his eyes to the damage Durell had caused.

"We need to move right now."

"What is that?" Sean asked.

"Halon system," Thomas answered. "Generally, not an issue when used to suppress a fire. But your boss ruptured the pipeline, and now it's flooding the entire deck without a hope in hell of stopping. Soon enough, we'll have the entire station's supply in this one section."

"In other words, we need to get our butts down to the processing station," Charity said.

"No arguments here," Sean replied.

All at once, they moved for the nearest stairwell.

CHAPTER 13

"Aren't you glad I brought along my Phoenix-M2 Plasma Rifles?" Howard said to Thomas as he entered the processing station.

Thomas took a minute to look at his, and instead of giving the engineer a well-deserved compliment, he decided to stay true to his personality.

"Would be nice if it could hit anything that's more than two inches in front of me."

Howard sighed and shook his head. *Typical.*

"It's more than two inches."

"Doesn't feel like it when the target's rushing you," Charity said. "Especially if they can take several hits."

"Oh, thanks. I see you're taking his side," Howard quipped. "You know, I could invent real life lightsabers, and you still would find something to complain about."

"Damn right I would," Charity said. "Especially since you'd probably leave out the purple ones."

Howard raised a finger. "That's unique to Mace, okay?"

"Like it matters," Renee said. "Howard would probably produce a bunch of yellow ones."

"There's nothing wrong with yellow lightsabers," the engineer responded. "Just because we haven't seen them until recent additions doesn't make it innately bad."

As the banter went on, Thomas took notice of a bemused look on Sean Regal's face, as well as the four station employees.

"Yes, this is how we roll," he said, answering their unspoken question.

"Speaking of rolling," Durell said in a loud and firm tone, "we need to get the hell out of here."

Sean froze.

Thomas knew the facial expression. The guy was not used to hearing the angst in his commander's voice. Even in tight situations, Durell was the kind of guy who kept a level head. But here, he appeared ready to jump in that submarine and get out of here himself.

"We're gonna need a few minutes," Charity said. She walked over to where Spencer was seated. "It's gonna be a long trip with this guy's foot mangled like this. Can someone get me a med kit?"

Renee got on it.

As the doctor worked on Spencer, Thomas took the opportunity to speak with May Dyner and her fellow crewmembers.

"You guys alright?"

"Yes," May replied. "Thank you."

"The rest of us aren't," Brian called out. "Eight of us are dead. Nice work there, Captain Rodney, for putting us in that position."

Feinstein turned around, his brow furrowed. "Beg your pardon? You suggesting they should've let us sit in there to rot?"

"And weren't you coming down here with or without us anyway?" Howard said. "Without us, you'd all be lunch. Whether it be for the sharks or the lobster-millipede things—whatever they are."

Moses tucked his chin down and covered his mouth to 'cough'. "Some elite security force Brom-Caylen employs."

"As appreciative as I am of your efforts so far, and much as I find this back and forth entertaining…" Alexandra said. "I'd appreciate a solution to one issue that's worrying me." She pointed at the *Corman*. "Is it just me, or is that thing damaged?"

"That's correct," Howard said. "Arriving here was not without its problems. There's a big fish outside and it's looking to eat anything that moves."

"No kidding," Charity said while she stitched Spencer's foot. "It's the deepest species of shark I've ever seen. And since its home was contaminated by the meteorite, it probably survived this long by feeding off the smaller sharks and the crustaceans. I saw the swimmerets on their hind sections. They're definitely aquatic."

"Figured that part out from the fact we're almost three miles beyond where the sun don't shine," Renee remarked.

Charity shot her a look. "Point is; you're gonna have a field day getting us out of here."

"We might just have to wing it," Durell said.

Thomas stared at the security leader, noting every aspect of his body language.

"Can't just 'wing it'," he said. "Not when we have a disabled sub. The *McQueen's* good, but it can't tow that thing all the way to the surface. Plus, there's the issue of space. Both subs altogether can only hold thirteen people. We've got fourteen. So, unless one of you plans to draw straws, we need to figure out a solution."

"Are there any other subs?" Renee asked the crew members. "Anything in the garage we can hook up to?"

"I couldn't tell ya," May said. "I know most of the lifeboats have been deployed. I'm not sure if there are any left."

Howard cleared his throat. That sound, plus the look on his face, confirmed there was good news and bad news to be shared.

"Which one you want to hear first?"

"Just spit them both out," Thomas said.

"Good news: there is another lifeboat," Howard said. "Bad news…"

"Let me guess," Renee said. "It's far away from where we are."

Howard made a nervous grin, then put his hand to a marking on the computer's map of the station. "North Section, A Deck, Quartermaster's office. There's nothing on the automated log regarding deployment. That doesn't mean it wasn't used after the system went down, but still…"

"It's worth a try," Charity said. "Frankly, it's our only chance."

"It beats attempting to tow the *Corman*," Sean added.

"On that note, we can try and distract the big shark," Renee said. "Those lifeboats can hold quite a few people, yes?"

"Eight," May confirmed.

Renee snapped her fingers. "Perfect. We can get them there, get it set up to launch, then make sure big ol' *Bruce* out there is distracted. Once he's out of the way, they can launch. We've still got one torpedo left; we might be able to plant a shot right in the back of his throat."

"A lot of 'mights' in there," Charity said.

Renee's expression shriveled. "You have a better idea?"

Charity thought for a moment, then conceded with a shrug. "Unfortunately, I don't. All that I can think of right now are vacation spots."

"Yeah?" Howard said. "What's on your mind? Mai Tais in Hawaii? Snowboarding in Utah? Eating pasta in Venice, Italy?"

"Any one of those sounds good enough to me," Charity replied. "Just as long as there are no monsters. And plenty of alcohol."

May stepped forward, her face moist with a fresh coat of sweat. Her teeth were clenched in a way that suggested she could not even form a nervous smile properly.

"Something the matter?" Renee asked.

"Um…" May ran her hand over her forehead. "About the shark… were you aware of the other big one?"

The large room went quiet.

Howard tilted his head forward. "*Other* big one?"

"The answer's no," Thomas said, in a hurry to get to the point. "We've only encountered a pack of sharks out there. We killed the smaller ones, and barely managed to avoid the big daddy of the bunch."

"Or momma," Renee added.

"Yeah, whatever," Thomas moaned. "Are you saying there's something else out there?"

All four of the station workers nodded.

"Those bug-crab things?" Feinstein said. "They're just the little ones."

"Their momma is out there," Moses said. "And she's not friendly at all."

"The mega shark knows firsthand," May added. "Those two were butting heads when this thing started. I think it has a lot to do with the latest payload we brought in from the dig. You see, that rock with the mineral contained a crap-ton of eggs—*her* eggs. Obviously, they hatched in here and now occupy the place."

Thomas strutted to the *McQueen* and put his head against its hull. "Great. Lovely. Why did I take this job?"

Another few moments of silence filled the room.

"Because she's hot?"

Everyone looked at Moses, who was looking at Charity. He noticed the attention on him, most of which was disparaging.

Over in the corner, Archer watched with raised eyebrows, officially distracted from the rifle magazine he had brought to enjoy during the submarine ride.

Moses smiled nervously. "Just say'n…"

For an awkward moment, the guy had done the impossible: the entire group had actually forgotten about the man-eating crustaceans moving about in the station and the giant shark swimming outside.

Charity touched her chin, then suddenly gasped. "Holy crap! We're gonna need to do something about that!"

Now everyone was looking at her.

"Beg your pardon?!" Renee exclaimed.

"Huh… oh, NO! Not *that*… I was thinking out loud. May had said there were eggs in the fragment they brought in. It stands to reason there are others. The mother might have a nest over there."

"Oh, gosh," Sean groaned. "There might end up being hundreds of those things."

"Unless we destroy the nest," Thomas said.

"We need heat," Charity said. She noticed Moses' inappropriate grin. "Real heat! The kind that goes 'bang'." She cringed, realizing she made his smile widen. "Oh, for heaven's sake! I'm talking explosives! Geez, maybe we should leave him here."

Moses grin flipped upside down. "What? No! I think you're right on the money with the banging… BLASTING!" Now he was the one sweating. "Um, we have explosives in the garage. They should be okay. Their cannisters are designed to withstand the water pressure."

Thomas turned his eyes to Renee. "You think you can move some of the explosives over there?"

"And detonate them with my torpedo?" she completed his question. "Absolutely."

"Fantastic," Thomas said. "We've got a plan. First thing's first: let's get ready to move you guys to the lifeboat. Given the number of those things in the station, we're not likely to have an uneventful trip."

"Wait! Hold on!" Charity said. "Not to sound insensitive, but the creatures are in South Section, where Revere Team were taken down, bless their souls. Can't we just seal that entire section off?"

"Funny you ask," Howard said. He tapped on the keyboard of his computer. "I tried to do that very thing once I heard you guys were clear of the tunnel, but the system won't respond."

"Maybe something's off with your computer," Renee said.

"No, I don't think so." Howard brought up a schematic showing all passageways in the station. "Everything's wide open. It wasn't that way when we came in."

Thomas looked over at Durell. "You know anything about this?"

Durell shook his head. "You think I *want* those things free-roaming this place while I'm trapped in here?"

Thomas looked over at Sean, studying the corporal's expression while he glared at his superior.

Something was up.

Whatever it was, it did not go according to plan.

"We'll discuss it later," Thomas said. "Let's get ready to head back to North Section."

CHAPTER 14

Durell glanced at his watch. Twenty-four minutes until detonation. And with the bugs infesting South Section, there was no hope of going back there and disarming them.

The Raptor Pack guys were busy doing their own thing in preparation for moving to the lifeboat. The station's crew members were keeping close to them, clearly preferring Raptor Pack's presence to the company's own security team. On its face, it was an insult. But in Durell's eye, it was a small favor.

He moved over to where Spencer was seated, coming off as a leader checking in on his injured subordinate.

"How's that foot?"

"It's seen better days," Spencer replied.

"Roger that," Durell said. He glanced at the others, making sure he would not be overheard. "Well done with providing me intel."

"No problem," Spencer said. "Corporal Regal was quick to spill the beans. They know everything. And, as you can imagine, they're planning on exposing Brom-Caylen as soon as they're topside."

Durell smiled. "Not gonna happen." He followed the statement with a wink, silently confirming to Spencer that the trap was set.

Spencer made a deviant grin, which quickly shrank as he noticed the timer on Durell's watch.

"Wait… what about us?"

By now, Durell was motioning to Brian and Laurie to join him. At this point, he did not care much if Sean was privy to the plan. However, the corporal saw what was going on and decided to join in.

"What's going on?" he asked.

Durell pursed his lips, his bitterness towards the corporal on full display. It was only because of the shortage of time that he did not bother with chastising Sean for revealing company plans.

"Listen up, everyone: I've got charges set in South Section. Every airtight door in this station is locked open, meaning an implosion from the south will depressurize the rest of the facility. The automatic timer set in. We've got twenty-three minutes to get out of here."

Brian gulped. "That's not a lot of time."

"And a lot to do during that time," Laurie added. "We're talking getting the crew over to the lifeboat and some of us coming all the way back here…"

"Unless…" Durell kept his voice low and double-checked to make sure he was not overheard by the others, "…When we get to the lifeboat, we take out the Raptor Pack guys."

Brian winced. "Whoa."

"You sure about going that far?" Laurie whispered.

"If those guys get up there with proof of what was going on, the entire company goes down. We have to destroy this place. It's already been approved by the top brass. But we're short on time. We're down to twenty-two minutes. I need you knuckleheads on board."

After a moment of consideration, Spencer, Brian, and Laurie nodded. There was a hint of reluctance in the latter two's expression, but all the same, they were willing to go along with his scheme.

Sean, on the other hand, looked at his four fellow security operatives as though they had horns growing out of their heads.

"You sons of bitches," he growled. "Those guys saved all of our asses. And you're repaying them with *this*?!"

Durell bared his teeth and waved a hand frantically. "Keep your damn voice down, will ya? We're committed to this, one way or another. You better get on board, Corporal, or you'll be left down here with them."

"Yeah?" Sean replied. "Awfully convenient that everything is in place, and that no warning was given prior to now. It's almost as though you planned on rigging the place to blow, and jumping ship with Revere Team while the rest of us were left in ignorance. The station would implode and nobody would know."

Everyone's eyes were on Durell now.

He maintained a stern expression, unfazed by the assessment by Sean.

"Believe what you want. Fact is, we're pressed for time and need to make a move."

The others were quiet for another few moments.

Following a sigh, Spencer leaned over to him. "We can shoot them now and take their fancy guns. They won't see it coming."

"Might be best," Brian whispered. "That way we can double our pace to North Section. Those guys will want to exercise caution the whole way. Not that I blame them, but given the circumstances…"

"Yeah, that might be the best option," Laurie concurred.

Sean was beet red. "You…" He could not even form words. In his eyes, these men he had worked with for years proved themselves to be less than human. At least the crustaceans and sharks had a clear, understandable motive. They were predators. They killed to feed. But Durell? He killed so company secrets could remain intact. A company that would throw him under the bus the minute he outlived his usefulness.

"Something the matter?" Thomas called over to them.

Durell grimaced. Of all the moments, it was this one where the G.O.R.E. Sector guy took notice of their little meeting.

He burned his eyes into Sean, warning him not to say anything.

Fingers slowly slipped into the trigger guards, the four soldiers ready to commit to the plan right here and now.

Thomas did not like what he was seeing. He had worked alongside enough dirtbags in his career to know when a double-cross was on the horizon. Sean Regal was looking him in the eye, the only guy to display some measure of humanity in this otherwise dreadful group.

His own finger entered the trigger guard of his gun. The rest of Raptor Pack watched intently, each one readying their weapons. Though they did not know exactly what was on the security team's minds, the silent unease in the room may as well have been a blaring siren.

The uneasiness reached new heights as the silence was interrupted by a sound within the walls.

Tap! Tap! Tap! Tap! Tap! Tap! Tap! Tap!

All fourteen people looked in all directions. It was a dreadful sound that was very familiar, especially for Durell, who had recently experienced what came after.

"Oh, sh—"

Panels flew open. From the newly-created openings, a dozen crustaceans swarmed the processing station.

The security team dispersed, with Spencer hobbling on his one good foot to keep up with Durell.

Suppressed gunfire mixed with the sound of ravenous hisses, and soon, screams.

The first scream came from Laurie. One of the crustaceans came down right on top of him, flattening the soldier against the deck. Having lost possession of his firearm, he found himself staring directly into a gruesome assortment of teeth and mouthparts. A foul odor drifted from the back of that corkscrew set of jaws.

Sniveling, he pushed both hands against the creature's face to keep it from making its fatal bite. It was an effort which only served to give the monster a new target. Instead of biting on his neck, it went for one of those hands.

Laurie howled in agony, his right arm quickly consumed down to the elbow. His scream deteriorated into a gasp as both forelegs plunged into his chest, perforating his lungs.

Bright blue flashes coursed through the station as plasma bolts gradually reduced the enemy numbers.

Archer kept his shots fast and accurate, focusing on headshots. Never once did he miss. If the projectile did not immediately penetrate the target's skull, it at least severed one if not both of its antennae, thus throwing the creature into a confused tantrum.

A smell of cooked meat permeated the station.

Renee and Howard put themselves between the threat and the crew members; the engineer praying his technology lived up to the praise he had given it. Blazing blue bolts tore into one of the frightening beasts, separating one of its arms from its torso. As it whipped into a frenzy, he continued hitting it with more shots, thoroughly cutting it down to size.

Thomas and Charity were advancing to the *McQueen*, where three of the creatures were attempting to cut through the hull, believing the big thing to be a large organism full of tasty flesh.

Two of the creatures were picked off easily, their heads shriveling from an intense heat that cooked their brains. The third coiled its lower half on the sub and turned to the human attackers, ready to spring.

Charity hit its lower segments with a rapid burst. Instead of launching at them, the creature's baking muscles flung it sideways in an awkward manner. As it hit the floor, Thomas took out both of its eyes with two consecutive shots. Spewing steam and blood from its face, the crustacean waved its upper body and slashed its talons wildly.

A third hit to the face put its tantrum to an end, thus sparing the *McQueen* from any significant damage.

"No! No! Get back, YOU NASTY FREAK!"

Bullets passed near Thomas' temple, forcing him to duck. Near the east wall, Brian had gone mad in his failed attempt to repel two of the creatures. He waved his rifle muzzle left and right, his eyes wide and the skin on his face rippling with a storm of tension.

Two of the crustaceans advanced on him.

Click! Click! Click!

Even with the dreaded sounds of an empty gun, Brian continued squeezing the trigger. It was a split-second before the monsters lunged when he finally found the self-control to get a new one. By then, it was too late.

The horrid beasts took him down and went to work hacking him up with their deadly talons.

Rifle rounds sparked against their exoskeletons. Approaching from the left was Sean Regal, rifle shouldered, its mag getting emptied in an effort to save his teammate.

The two crustaceans lifted their talons and mandibles from Brian, reacting to the pelting of pointy lead against their bodies.

Sean ejected his empty magazine and slammed a fresh one home. He put his eye to the scope and leveled the red dot with one of those huge eyes.

BANG!

Sean lurched, his chest rupturing from within. He looked down at himself, seeing a river of blood freefalling down his front, and dropped to his knees.

Thomas and Charity looked to the sound of the gunshot.

At the stairwell exit stood Durell with his rifle pointed at the corporal. With a few of the creatures closing in on him, he grabbed ahold of Spencer and disappeared into the stairwell. A few gunshots echoed from within, followed by a crazed shriek from a crustacean in their path, and the thud of its body coming down the steps. It lay at the doorway, bleeding from both eyes.

Archer unloaded into the other two at the door, decapitating them with well-placed plasma shots.

Thomas and Charity closed in on the pair of crustaceans feeding on Brian and hollowed out their skulls with sweltering blue energy.

After completing the kills, they knelt by the dying Sean Regal. He was lying on his back now, hand on his exit wound, struggling for air.

"Hang on, Corporal," Thomas said.

"N-no," Sean moaned. "D-D-Durell…"

"Don't worry," Charity said. "We'll go after the bastard."

"No!" Sean wheezed. He managed to get a breath to speak as clearly and quickly as possible. "He's rigged the place to blow. That's why all the doors are locked open. He put bombs all over South Section. Twenty minutes until they blow."

Thomas and Charity looked at each other.

All of a sudden, it all made sense. Durell was attempting to cover the company's tracks, and bury them with it. One way or another, the meteorite sample would be lost with the wreckage, as would all available records of the experiments. There was no time to download anything and safely retrieve a sample of the particles. They needed to clear the area now.

That's what Durell was attempting to do. Going after him was useless. At best, they would find themselves in a firefight with the guy. Their only hope of getting out were the submersibles.

"Come on, Sean," Charity said. "Stay awake. Don't even think about dying on us."

He cracked a weak smile.

"Too late," he said in a raspy voice. "I'm sorry I was part of this. Those things are monsters. I wish I was part of G.O.R.E. Sector, saving the world, instead of helping to put it in danger… Please… Stop Brom-Caylen. Promise me…"

His jaw went slack and his eyelids drooped. Charity put her hand over his eyes and closed them. The poor guy had succumbed to his wound, his last moments spent haunted by the reality of whom he had been serving.

Thomas and Charity shared another glance. In turn, they also shared the same thought.

We promise, Sean.

They turned around and regrouped with the rest of Raptor Pack.

"What the hell was that?" Renee said. "Why'd Durell shoot him?"

"Because he wasn't going along with the scheme," Thomas said. "Durell rigged the place to blow. Sean said twenty minutes; probably down to nineteen by now. Durell's making his way for the lifeboat. We don't have a lot of options." He looked at the four company workers. "You four are gonna have to ride in the *Corman*. We still have a cable hooked up to it. We'll drag you guys out of here and hopefully make enough distance to be safe from the shockwave."

"Unfortunately, that doesn't solve the issue of getting them topside," Howard said.

Thomas looked at the schematic of the station, focusing on the garage layout. Within that structure was a loading bay where cargo was lifted to the station.

Charity watched his face while he thought. "I know that look."

"What look?" he asked.

"The one you get when you come up with a clever idea."

He pointed at himself. "I have a look?"

"Yeah," Renee chimed in. "It's like a TV show moment."

"Hmm." He eyeballed his team of oddball, yet elite squad of specialists. "Seems fitting, I guess."

"So, do you have an idea?" Howard asked.

"That I do."

CHAPTER 15

Captain Dennis Kelleway was in his quarters, having been stripped of all control of the surface station *Guardian* by the company roach Vinnie Gavel. He, and several other security personnel were moving through the station, downloading everything from the computers before purging.

Something was up; something above his paygrade. But Dennis was not an idiot. He knew what covering tracks looked like, and Vinnie's personnel were moving with haste to make sure there was nothing linking the *Guardian* to whatever was happening three miles below it.

The phone on his nightstand chimed.

He picked it up. "Kelleway here."

"Captain, this is Ken. I just received a transmission from the G.O.R.E. Sector team. They need our help, but Vinnie shut down the call."

"What do they need?" Dennis asked.

"They need the lift cable deployed," Ken said. *"One of the subs is disabled and the only way to get it out of danger is for us to hoist it. But Vinnie shut down the transmission. He doesn't know I'm calling you. He stepped out of the office for the moment, but he'll be back at any time."*

"Those damn psychos," Dennis muttered. Something happened at the *Scarlett Caldera* and Vinnie was attempting to cover it up. In doing so, he was condemning several people to death. "Hang on. I'll be right there."

He flung himself off the bunk and raced out the door.

When he arrived in the radio shack, he saw helicopters appearing on the horizon. They were nearing the flight deck, where a large crate full of the station's computers were being held.

A shutdown was in progress.

The crew of the *Crixus* were on edge. Weapons were on standby and the captain stood on the starboard bridge wing, continuously providing instructions to his men. It was safe to assume he had come to the same conclusion, and was taking measures to ensure no action would be taken against the vessel.

Dennis knew they had nothing to worry about. Should any of the men aboard the ship be asked to testify, all they would be able to say was unmarked crates were being offloaded. Aside from that, they had no clue what was going on.

Ken was seated at the main desk. Only the main computer was still present, as it could not be detached from the control console.

"Where's Vinnie?"

The door opened. The company rep hit the captain with a fierce glare.

"Right there," Ken quipped.

"What are you doing?" Vinnie barked.

Dennis knew the chances of a healthy discussion was out the window. He removed a key from his pants pocket and inserted it into the control console.

"Whoops."

He shifted the lever and deployed the cable.

***

Thomas held May's hand and helped lower her into the *Corman*. She looked at her coworkers inside the cramped quarters, then at the captain.

"Thanks."

"Not a problem," he said.

"Might be a dumb question, but is there anything I can do to help?" she asked.

"Give him your number," Feinstein joked.

"No. He's taken by the hot lady super-scientist," Moses replied.

Thomas stared, mouth agape, reminding himself they were on a clock. "Um, can you access the lift controls from the sub?"

"That I can," May said. "I'm familiar with the system."

"Perfect. Aside from that, keep the radio headphones on. Help us find those explosives so we can blow up the nest. Cable's on the way down. We'll have you out of here shortly."

"Thanks again," May said.

She shut the hatch and sealed it from inside.

Thomas turned around to run to the *McQueen*. Standing in his way was Charity, staring with a grin on her face.

"Heck of a group we're saving."

"They certainly like to jump to conclusions," he responded. "Let's get the hell out of here."

They boarded the *McQueen* and sealed its hatch.

Renee was at the controls, ready to steer the powerful vehicle out of the loading bay.

The floor lowered into a vast and dark loading bay. The overhead sealed and pressurized, keeping the rest of the station safe while the subs deployed.

May filled the chamber with seawater, then lowered the ramp.

The ocean floor came into view, lit by the dim glow of the remaining perimeter lights.

Renee put the *McQueen* to work. "Here we go."

Towing the *Corman*, she exited the *Scarlett Caldera*. The weight of the disabled sub was quickly apparent, preventing the *McQueen* from going much faster than a snail's pace.

"How much time is left?" Charity asked.

"Roughly fifteen minutes," Thomas said.

"I hope that cable makes it down here in time," Renee said. "It's a little farther than dropping a fishing line into the local pond."

"I saw the winch up there on the *Guardian*," Howard said. "Trust me, that cable's coming down hard and fast like an anvil."

"Right now, I'd be more worried about our fish friend," Thomas said.

There were no readings on the sonar. So far, they appeared to be alone out here. In reality, they knew that was far from the case.

"You see the garage?" May said through the radio.

"Affirmative," Renee replied.

"On the east side is the loading dock. Usually it's covered, but it looks like the exterior has been destroyed. But if you can, bring us there. I might be able to use the Corman's utility arms to attach the cable."

"Sounds good," Renee said. "Hang on, guys. This might be a little bumpy."

With that said, she applied full power to the thrusters.

***

"Quit dragging your feet, damn it. We're running out of time."

"Pardon me, boss," Spencer groaned at Durell. "Sorry I have such a heavy foot."

They had reached the North Section and made a turn to locate a stairwell to take them to A Deck.

Spencer hopped on his one good leg, struggling to keep up with Durell.

They heard faint vibrations rippling from West Section. Durell stopped and looked back.

"That wasn't the water current," he said to himself.

"What was it?" Spencer asked, still clinging to him with one arm and using the other to point his rifle.

Durell sniggered. "Those suckers are making a run for it. That's alright. G.O.R.E. Sector won't leave without the *Corman*, and they won't be able to ascend while towing it. Being the 'good guys' comes at a price. The implosion will create a shockwave that'll take 'em all out. Assuming the shark doesn't get them first. On that note, they might be doing us a favor. They'll keep the big fish preoccupied while we get out of dodge."

Another sound—a *nearer* sound—erased his devilish grin and the confidence behind it.

Tapping sounds, coming from somewhere within the passageway, rapidly grew nearer.

"Boss?" Spencer whispered.

Durell turned northeast and pointed his flashlight at a group of misshapen mutants. There were five of them, spilling thick rivers of drool, swinging their scythe-like arms like demons emerging from a deep chasm.

"Boss, we're trapped!" Spencer said. "I don't think I can get around them!"

"I suppose not," Durell slurred.

The hairs on Spencer's neck raised on end. He looked at Durell in hopes that the betrayal he sensed was a figment of his imagination.

It wasn't, confirmed by the gunshot to his other leg. Spencer hit the deck, wailing in pain.

Durell made a run in the opposite direction of the passageway, following the perimeter northwest. Behind him, the deep-sea mutants closed in on Spencer.

He yelled maniacally and blasted away with his gun. It did no good; not for him, at least.

The next yells were full of pain.

Durell formed a new grin after locating another stairway. The guy proved useful as a distraction while he got to safety…precisely why he took the time and effort to drag him along.

As he explained to Spencer, being a good guy came at a price. What he didn't explain was it was the same way for being the bad guy. Except for the latter, the price was often paid by someone else.

Content with this fact, he moved to A Deck.

CHAPTER 16

"Nice work, Raptor Pack. We're on the cargo platform. You're clear to detach your tow cable."

May felt her companions bumping against the back of her pilot seat as they watched through the front visor. The *McQueen* reeled in its cable and began moving toward the wreckage that was once the eastern part of the garage.

It hovered over the disfigured mass that was once a glorious feat of architecture. Arms, ironically shaped like those of the crustaceans, began lifting pieces of rubble and pushed them aside.

From where they sat, the *McQueen* resembled an alien craft passing over a devastated town where it had laid waste. Its pilot rotated the craft forty degrees counterclockwise and sorted through what used to be the storage section.

"The explosives are silver in color, are about eight feet in length…"

Feinstein pushed May aside to take control of the microphone. "They look like giant beer bottles."

"I could use one of those myself," Renee said. She lifted a large slab of rubble and pushed it aside. *"I see some underwater digging equipment. Whoa! Is that a suit?"*

"State of the art," May said.

"Neat stuff. Iron Man type of stuff. I might need to try one of those things out. Howard, what are the odds you can build something like that?"

"Let him perfect plasma guns first," Thomas said.

Alexandra fidgeted in her seat. "Any chance they can hurry up? Not to sound ungrateful, but we are kinda on a clock."

"Ten minutes, give or take thirty seconds," Moses said.

"I'm not gonna impede on the way these guys work," May replied. "All I know for sure is that this is not their first rodeo."

"Ah-ha! Looks like I found us some beer bottle bombs!" Renee exclaimed.

The *McQueen* ascended several meters, with two of the explosives clutched in its arms.

"Even better," she continued. *"I'm getting a proximity alert. I think that cable is coming down."*

May checked her sub's computer. "Yep, I see it too."

Her three companions cheered.

Moses pumped a fist. "Nice!"

"We're almost out of here!" Alexandra declared. "Praise the Lord!"

Beep!

"Hey…" Feinstein leaned over May's shoulder and looked at the sonar screen. "What's that?"

A second blip emerged from the west. It was an object of immense size, moving at great speed.

May sucked in a breath. "Oh, no." She pressed the transmitter. "Raptor Pack! It's coming!"

"Copy that, Corman. We see it. Hold on to your butts, guys. We're in for a ride."

A whoosh of water shook the *Corman* and a massive shadow passed through the glow of the station's lights.

May bit on her finger, her entire body numb at the incredible, yet frightening sight. The shark was maybe ninety feet in length, dark grey in color, save for the white of her eight-inch teeth. Her mighty size did not impede her speed, for she moved at cheetah speed.

The *McQueen* ascended quickly, allowing the shark to pass underneath it. Renee engaged the throttle, moving the sub in the opposite direction.

The shark turned, her massive eyes glistening in the glow of the station's lights. A sway of her enormous caudal fin sent her after the mechanical foe. Like a huge torpedo locked onto a target, she moved in for the kill.

Renee steered the vessel to starboard and engaged a flare. The shark did not fall for it this time. It passed the haunting red light and continued on course.

"Oh, not fair!"

The sub's next move was to make a plunge. It barely worked, the shark's underside grazing the propellers as it passed overhead.

A looping motion put the *McQueen* back on an upward trajectory.

"Eight minutes," Moses warned.

"I'm sure they're aware," Alexandra said.

WHOOSH!

The shark passed near the *Corman*, causing Feinstein to squeal and duck. It moved up and right, performing a sharp turn to go after the *McQueen*.

Renee now had the sub facing the threat head-on.

A harpoon launched from one of its ports and struck the fish right in the nose. A blue strobe of energy, like a lightning bolt, coursed over its snout, resulting in a brief spasm. Twisting into a corkscrew motion, the shark nosedived into the seabed, kicking up a thick cloud of silt.

Its malfunction was over right away, and the shark was back to gaining altitude.

This time, it moved in a wide circle, keeping its left eye on the *McQueen*. It kept a distance of sixty feet from the vessel, gaining speed as it made more passes.

"They're not going to outrun it," Alexandra said.

"Can't stand toe-to-toe with it either," Moses added. "The thing's too big. I'm not even sure that torpedo of theirs would do the trick. Not unless they shot it directly into its mouth."

"They need that for the nest," May said. "We need to get the thing off their back."

The other three workers looked at her as if she had gone mad.

"We?" Feinstein said. "Not sure if you noticed, but this tin can is not exactly in fighting shape."

May watched the shark. It was stretching its jaws, readying itself for a critical bite.

She combed through many controls on the instrument panel until she found the one she was looking for.

Flares.

She pressed the button.

Several flashes of red streaked from both sides of the *Corman,* casting a bright radiance over the trench.

The shark stopped its attack short and turned around to inspect the source of visual stimulation. It slowed its speed and tilted its nose fifteen degrees downward… right at the *Corman.*

Feinstein cleared his throat, alarmed by the gradual decrease in space between them and the fish.

"Well, it *sorta* worked."

The beast proceeded to come at them, no longer interested in the flares.

May gripped her seat. It appeared the creature was aware that the flares had come from the *Corman* and did not belong to some other deep-sea organism.

"Oh, hell…"

"Hang on, guys," Renee said in a chirpy tone.

Another harpoon struck the shark, its tip grazing its tail. The brief shock electrical jolt was enough to draw it away from the *Corman.*

A sharp turn created a gust of water that nearly rolled the sub onto its back.

By now, the cable was within a hundred meters. It was directly above them, just a few moments away from lifting them to safety.

The big fish moved in on the *McQueen.*

Renee had it in reverse, taking the sub closer to the *Scarlett Caldera.*

"The hell is she doing?" May said.

They watched the sub come within a few feet of South Section.

"Here, fishy fishy," Renee taunted.

The shark thrust its tail and tripled its speed in the blink of an eye. Jaws parted and eyes rolled back, all strength committed to devastating the sub.

Renee banked to port, bypassing the huge fish.

Still moving at rapid speed, it rammed face-first into the station.

BAM!

It was an impact devastating enough to form a large crater in the side of the structure.

The shark twirled to the seafloor, twitching its jaws and tail, blood wafting from its nostrils. It was still alive, but had a massive headache to say the least.

"Dang," an impressed May said. "Nice work, Renee."

"G.O.R.E. Sector didn't hire me just for my good looks."

"Nah, that was the biologist lady," Moses quipped.

May looked at him. "Give it up, dude. You don't have a snowball's chance in hell."

The cable came down on the top of their sub.

Renee brought the *McQueen* over, its arms still attached. *"Hang on. I'll get that for ya."* She hovered over the *Corman* and used the digits to secure the cable to the cleats up top. *"You're good to go. Make a call to the Guardian."*

"Copy that," May said. "Don't take too long, alright. You have maybe six minutes to get out of here."

"Eh, who's counting?"

Thomas Rodney peered into the cockpit at Renee. "Um, I am."

"Yeah, me too," Charity said.

"You can include me in that," Howard added.

Archer checked his watch. "Especially since you're going so slow, we may as well have hired a North Korean pilot."

Renee looked over her shoulder at him, mouth agape. "Oh! You did not just go there!"

She put the sub to its maximum speed and located the two explosives she dug out. The claws secured the two bombs to the underside while she turned west and soared through the darkness to the dig site.

As they moved away from the garage, they witnessed the *Corman* lift off the platform. Their journey to safety had begun.

The *McQueen* passed over three quarters of a mile of a desolate trench before arriving at the massive crater that was the dig site.

It was located near the trench wall on the north side, burrowing down at a forty-five-degree angle. From far away, it almost resembled an insect nest in a yard, with the outer edges elevated from deeper sediment being discarded over the surface. Tracks marked the ground where underwater excavation vehicles went to work. Chunks of rock were scattered, resulting from concentrated explosive charges.

Renee steered the *McQueen* to the mouth of the cave and performed a scan. Readings showed that the thing went over five hundred feet deep.

"I've got bio signs," she announced.

Charity moved to take a look at the computer monitor. On the screen, they looked like bundles of orange grapes. In reality, they were crustacean eggs. Hundreds of them. Maybe over a thousand.

"You think those explosives will be enough?" she asked.

"Each one of these contains enough bombs to devastate this entire cave," Renee answered.

Charity nodded, satisfied with that answer.

Renee took the sub deep inside.

"Four minutes," Thomas announced.

"Yes, yes, yes," Renee said. "We're far enough away from the station to survive the shockwave. I wouldn't worry. We're practically out of the woods. Something would have to seriously go awry at this point to set us back…"

***

Durell scrambled to get the controls functional. The lifeboat had required some nitrogen for pressurization before launch. Departing without it would do him no more good than standing around waiting for the bombs to go off. He'd pop like a grape halfway to the surface.

The system was in the green, and with four minutes to go, he had just enough time to get to a safe distance.

He entered the lifeboat and launched.

The teepee-shaped vessel was lifted through an inner airlock and into a launch tube. Water filled the compartment, and after a few moments, the outer airlock doors parted.

The lifeboat was ejected into the open ocean.

Durell sported a triumphant smile, watching through the porthole at the wreckage that was the station's perimeter. A blight white light blinked from the lifeboat's beacon, brightly flashing over the station and everything around it.

He saw the *Corman* slowly ascending on a cable. Underneath it was the garage, or rather, what was left of it.

Movement caught his eye. A cigar-shaped object thrashed on the seabed near the South Section. A flash of the lifeboat's beacon gave view of the crescent shape of an enormous caudal fin.

Durell's throat tightened. He prayed the shark was on the verge of death, perhaps fatally injured somehow by Raptor Pack. It was lying on the seabed, after all. Such a thing was not normal for a shark, right?

"Yeah, you lay there," Durell said. "Dumb fish."

The tail slapped the ground, kicking up silt. Strobing lights reached its eyes as the lifeboat towered over the station.

As though rejuvenated by a defibrillator, the shark shot off the bottom and darted upward to the source of light.

Durell took in the sight of numerous teeth and a bright red throat behind them.

"Oh, shit."

The jaws struck the lifeboat and compressed it.

BOOM!

***

"Whoa!" Feinstein yelled.

The *Corman* was thirty feet off the platform when May Dyner noticed movement coming from the top of the North Section. By the time they identified it to be the last lifeboat, the shark had revived and went straight to the flashing beacon. Durell's betrayal and subsequent quest for freedom had officially led to his undoing.

"Couldn't have happened to a nicer guy," Moses remarked.

The shark turned, spitting wreckage from its mouth. Following the sounds of vibrations, it moved in to inspect the *Corman.*

"Oh, you've got to be kidding me," May gasped. All of a sudden, she could relate to the bait she had placed on the end of a fishing line during her childhood years. She pressed the radio transmitter. "Raptor Pack! The shark's back up and moving. And he's showing a particular interest in us."

***

"We're on our way. Hang tight," Thomas responded.

Renee placed the second charge in the batch of eggs, then reversed the sub out of the mine.

"Piece of cake," she said. She locked on to one of the bombs, armed her final torpedo, and let it fly.

The bird struck its target and triggered a triple detonation: its own, and those from the two mining bombs.

A rush of water spewed from the mouth of the cave, carrying thick clouds of silt, silky strands of ravaged egg sacks, and chunks of rock.

Renee, after backing the *McQueen* farther away from the blast, clapped her hands and whooped.

"Another one bites the dust! Technically, another *thousand* bite the dust. Leave it to me to eradicate a nest of unholy pests."

"That's great and all," Charity said, "but where's the big one? Those eggs didn't lay themselves. Mommy's got to be around somewhere."

Renee waved her hand dismissingly. "Eh! Maybe she skipped town."

A proximity alert flashed on the screen. Charity glared at it, then at Renee.

"Or was out for errands while we broke into her house."

The glow of the *McQueen's* spotlights embraced the enormous, caterpillar shape of the oncoming threat.

The mother had the same general shape as her offspring, though with two additional arms and much longer legs and swimmerets. She moved along the seafloor, her massive arms appearing like spider legs as she approached what was once her burrow. Her antennae wavered, picking up traces of the devastated nest, as well as the water distortions made from the vessel that did the deed.

Huge mouthparts expanded underneath two bulging black eyes. Her body made squiggly motions in a similar manner as a moray eel, lifting her off the bottom. Intensified motions carried her towards the submersible, and thanks to the assisting force from the swimmerets, she picked up speed quickly.

She was equal to the shark's size and mass, and by the looks of it, its aggression as well.

Charity pointed her thumb at Renee. "She did it."

The lieutenant spun the *McQueen* one-hundred-and-eighty degrees and sped for the *Scarlett Caldera.* Behind it, the mother crustacean kept pace, her massive forelegs skimming the bottom.

The sub's computer continued blaring its alarm, warning its pilot of the massive organism on its six. Renee smashed the alarm button, switching it off.

"How they expect me to think with that racket in my ear is beyond me," she grumbled.

"Guys! I hope you're close! The shark is following us up. I think it's about to move in for a bite."

"Hang on," Renee said.

She launched some flares from both sides, lighting up the dark trench with their red strobes.

A new proximity alert blared, this time coming from the east.

"It's moving away. It sees your flares... We see you too! Nice work, Raptor Pack... wait... holy crap!"

Obviously they saw the mother crustacean following the sub. She continued the chase, undistracted by the bright red balls of light streaming from her victim.

Only when she came within proximity to an enemy she despised even more did the mother slow down.

The chase was over, the horrible crime forgotten for now. She was a territorial beast, but there was no true emotional connection to her lost eggs. If anything, they were meant to serve her much like ants did for their royal queen. In order to raise her empire, she needed domination over the territory.

Coming after her was the greatest obstacle to that ambition, moving towards her with equal aggression and desire for supremacy over the trench.

With both titans approaching from fore and aft, Renee banked to starboard and let the two beasts hash out their differences.

They collided with a thunderous clap that spewed an intense shockwave across the station. Two bodies became one, the crustacean's arms wrapping around the shark's body and pinning it tight to drive home those huge spurs.

The fish twisted into a corkscrew motion, taking itself and its opponent into the seafloor. They landed with a heavy *THUMP* and rolled for nearly a hundred feet before the mother lost her grip.

Multiple swipes of the caudal fin propelled the fish out of her reach. It circled back with a sharp left turn until its snout was pointed right at her.

The crustacean was standing upright, her upper half rising high like a Kodiak bear. She extended her arms and prepared to engage the fish directly.

Doubling its speed, the shark moved in for the kill.

BAM!

It struck like a battering ram, driving the mother crustacean on her back.

Her arms coiled, one of them securing a grip on the shark's right pectoral fin, preventing it from moving off without dragging her along. She pulled herself closer to the thick grey flesh and put her mandibles to work.

Horrid tools, designed for savaging the tough armor of rival crustaceans, made easy work of the shark's flesh. Clouds of blood spewed in the white glow of the station's lights, transforming their radiance into a hellish red color.

The fish twisted and freed itself from her jaws, then performed a wide swing with its tail. She absorbed the blow with her face and, for the second time in a row, was knocked on her back.

Again, the shark circled back to make a kill. This time, it anticipated the slicing motion of its opponent's forelegs, and adjusted its strategy accordingly.

It tilted itself sideways and passed over the crustacean, clamping its jaws down on one of her arms. Its massive biteforce combined with the intense momentum resulted with a resounding *CRACK*, and the spewing of blood from the mother's shoulder socket where her arm was removed from.

Like an insect dying on a sidewalk, she waved her remaining arms and all eighty of her legs in agony.

The shark moved in another semicircle, discarding the severed limb like a disposable coffee cup.

Above both of them was the *McQueen*, carefully monitoring the situation while moving to a safe distance. The *Corman* had now ascended five hundred feet and was well on its way to safety.

"Less than one minute until detonation," Howard announced.

"Hold here," Thomas said to Renee. "We have to see how this plays out."

"Should we place bets?" Renee asked.

"Are you kidding me?" Charity said. Her embittered look softened, and she reached into her wallet. "I got a hundred bucks here. I'd say the shark is gonna pull this one off."

"A hundred on Big Momma," Renee replied. "She's plenty angry and still has plenty of fight left in her."

"No way," Howard said. "It's not the first time those two have gone at it. They're both wounded. I'd put two hundred bucks that they part ways and we'll be stuck figuring out a way to come back down here and eliminate them."

Everyone looked to Archer. He sat, arms crossed, shaking his head.

"Captain's plan will work," he said.

"Yeah... for the survivor," Renee said. "Look at them freaks. Someone's about to lose their head. The survivor will get caught in the blast."

"Considering the massive blood loss from both of them, I consider that highly likely," Charity added.

"Two hundred bucks, from both myself and Archer," Thomas announced. He looked at the sniper for approval, which he received by a typical nod.

"You're on," Renee said.

Howard looked at his timer. "We're at zero."

Everyone braced for an explosion which could come at any moment. None came.

"Well, it was an estimate," Thomas said. "I didn't have direct access to Durell's clock."

"That, or the timer never engaged," Howard said. He

made a 'tisk' sound and shook his head like a teacher scolding a flunking student. "Should've taken that into consideration, Cap."

More vibrations traveled through the water as the two giants tussled in the glow of the *McQueen's* bright spotlights. The crustacean slashed her remaining arms like swords, lacerating the shark's face. It turned sharply to reposition, once again striking her face with its tail. This time, she managed to keep from falling over.

The shark made some distance and pointed its snout at her once more. Waving its caudal fin, it made another run.

The mother took a defensive stance, ready to absorb the blow.

BAM!

The shark took her off the seafloor and smashed her against the steel wall of South Section.

Though pinned and with her exoskeleton cracked, she continued clawing at her enemy, slicing the shark's back and neck. The shark ignored the pain and bit ferociously, separating one of her antennae before clamping its jaws on another of her arms.

Then, in the blink of an eye, a thunderous *BOOM* shook the trench. The *Scarlett Caldera* crumpled into itself and disappeared into a tremendous cloud of dust and rock.

A shockwave expanded from the epicenter in a perfect ring, tearing up the seabed and anything on it.

Renee brought the *McQueen* farther up, shaking in her seat as the shockwave reached the vessel.

From where the team watched, it resembled a heavy artillery explosion, easily wiping out the surrounding area.

After several moments, the turbulence ceased. Renee ran a diagnostic of the vessel and blew a sigh of relief after finding no signs of damage.

"We're okay," she said.

"Yeah, but what about the monsters?" Howard asked.

The sub slowly moved to the pile of rubble that had once been the *Scarlett Caldera*. By now, it was a heap of scrap metal, no more advanced than the piles of rusted cars in a regular junkyard.

Over the next several minutes, the silt dissipated.

Renee panned the spotlights back and forth until finding the shriveled heaps of flesh that were the corpses of the shark and crustacean.

"Oh, come on!"

"Wait…" Charity said. "It's technically possible the mother had her head crushed by the shark's jaws before the implosion occurred."

"By that logic, it's reasonable to assume the shark took a talon to the brain," Renee argued.

"Maybe they…" Howard bit his tongue, knowing there was no logical argument to support his bet. "I mean, it took a few minutes to get a visual. Maybe they survived the implosion and finished the fight right after."

All three of them looked to Thomas and Archer.

The pair sat victoriously, the sniper gracing them with a rare smile.

"You know, I like you better when you're antisocial," Renee said. She turned her eyes to Thomas. "And you! Shame on you for allowing your team members to gamble while on the job!"

"Yeah," Charity said. "We're supposed to be doing serious work. Yet, you allow us to commit this sinful act."

"Only way you can redeem yourself, Cap, is to not accept the money," Howard added.

They watched with hopeful eyes. That hope was soon crushed just like the *Scarlett Caldera* when the captain grinned at them.

"Yeah, nice try," he said. "That's what you get for using my account to buy those blackmail *Star Wars* helmets."

Howard groaned. "Black *Series*."

Renee faced forward and resumed their ascent to the *Guardian*. "Well, in that case, I'm wearing mine on the next mission."

CHAPTER 17

Golden sunlight warmed the *McQueen* as it was lifted onto the *Crixus.* When the five members of Raptor Pack exited the sub and stepped on the main deck, they looked to the several helicopters departing from the station's flight deck.

Dennis Kelleway stood outside the radio shack. Next to him was a stern-looking Vinnie Gavel, who watched G.O.R.E. Sector with red-hot eyes.

The *Corman* was successfully brought out of the water and onto the cargo deck. Its four occupants were safely brought out by some of the security personnel, who quickly escorted them to one of the choppers.

Some protests could be heard from May Dyner, who looked over at the *Crixus* in hopes of interference.

Thomas felt the urge to head over there and start exchanging blows with the armed men around her. The company was acting fast in its effort to cover up its wrongdoings, and part of that was getting those surviving crewmembers to an undisclosed location. There, they would probably be bribed… or threatened… in order to remain silent. A large sum of money would be given to them and they would, in all likelihood, be guaranteed a position in the company, complete with a generous retirement package in exchange for going along with the official narrative. Refusal would result in an 'accident' that would ensure their silence.

He would not blame them for going along with it. They were ordinary blue-collar workers who had no other way out. That did not lessen the anger building within him.

"Up until now, the only monsters we've had to worry about were actual oversized beasts," he said. "Now, we've got a different kind of monster; one that is well-financed and probably has some government backing."

"It's a whole new arms race," Charity said. "Leave it to our species to take advantage of something as terrible as the Ecclesiastes particle. At least Oppenheimer had the humanity to feel some regret for the creation of the atomic bomb."

"These people aren't the kind to feel remorse," Thomas said. "They're messing around with something they cannot control."

Charity crossed her arms over the gunnel. "What should we do?"

Thomas looked to the horizon. "We hunt. The *Scarlett Caldera* was only one of God-knows how many locations they have. Somewhere, at some point, they will slip up. And we'll know. That's when we'll take care of business."

Charity smiled. "Sounds good."

"First thing's first," Renee called to them. Thomas and Charity turned around and saw the rest of their team lifting beers from a cooler. "Another complete operation in the books. Gotta take part in the ritual."

Thomas chuckled. "We can always count on you to keep us on task, Lieutenant."

Together, they enjoyed their refreshment.

They would need it. In front of their eyes was a small component of what was likely a troublesome adversary.

Check out other great
Sea Monster Novels!

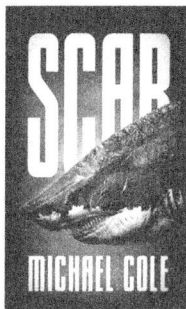

Michael Cole

SCAR

Scar is a killing machine. Born from DNA spliced between the extinct Megalodon and modern day Great White, he has a viciousness that transcends time. His evil is reflected in his eyes, his savagery in his two-inch serrated teeth, his ruthlessness in his trail of death. After escaping captivity, the killer shark travels to the island community Cross Point, where prey is in abundance. With an insatiable appetite, heightened senses, and skin impervious to bullets, Scar kills everything that crosses his path. His reign of terror puts him at war with the island sheriff, Nick Piatt. With the body count rising, Nick vows to protect his island community from the vicious threat. With the aid of a marine biologist, a rookie deputy, and a bad-tempered fisherman, Nick leads a crusade against Scar, as well as the ruthless scientist who created him.

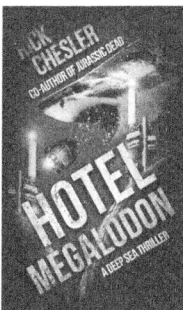

Rick Chesler

HOTEL MEGALODON

An underwater luxury hotel on a gorgeous tropical island is set for an extravagant opening weekend with the world watching. The only thing standing in the way of a first-rate experience for the jet-setting VIPs is an unscrupulous businessman and sixty feet of prehistoric shark. As the underwater complex is besieged by a marauding behemoth, newly minted marine biologist Coco Keahi must face off against the ancient predator as it rises from the deep with a vengeance. Meanwhile, a human monster has decided he would be better off if Coco were one of the creature's victims.

Check out other great

Sea Monster Novels!

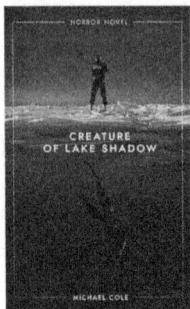

Michael Cole

CREATURE OF LAKE SHADOW

It was supposed to be a simple bank robbery. Quick. Clean. Efficient. It was none of those. With police searching for them across the state, a band of criminals hide out in a desolate cabin on the frozen shore of Lake Shadow. Isolated, shrouded in thick forest, and haunted by a mysterious history, they thought it was the perfect place to hide. Tensions mount as they hear strange noises outside. Slain animals are found in the snow. Before long, they realize something is watching them. Something hungry, violent, and not of this world. In their attempt to escape, they found the Creature of Lake Shadow.

C.J. Waller

PREDATOR X

When deep level oil fracking uncovers a vast subterranean sea, a crack team of cavers and scientists are sent down to investigate. Upon their arrival, they disappear without a trace. A second team, including sedimentologist Dr Megan Stoker, are ordered to seek out Alpha Team and report back their findings. But Alpha team are nowhere to be found – instead, they are faced with something unexpected in the depths. Something ancient. Something huge. Something dangerous. Predator X

Check out other great

Sea Monster Novels!

Matt James

SUB-ZERO

The only thing colder than the Antarctic air is the icy chill of death... Off the coast of McMurdo Station, in the frigid waters of the Southern Ocean, a new species of Antarctic octopus is unintentionally discovered. Specialists aboard a state-of-the-art DARPA research vessel aim to apply the animal's "sub-zero venom" to one of their projects: An experimental painkiller designed for soldiers on the front lines. All is going according to plan until the ship is caught in an intense storm. The retrofitted tanker is rocked, and the onboard laboratory is destroyed. Amid the chaos, the lead scientist is infected by a strange virus while conducting the specimen's dissection. The scientist didn't die in the accident. He changed.

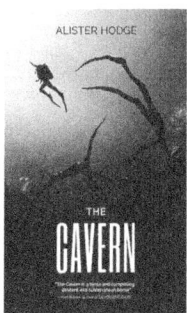

Alister Hodge

THE CAVERN

When a sink hole opens up near the Australian outback town of Pintalba, it uncovers a pristine cave system. Sam joins an expedition to explore the subterranean passages as paramedic support, hoping to remain unneeded at base camp. But, when one of the cavers is injured, he must overcome paralysing claustrophobia to dive pitch-black waters and squeeze through the bowels of the earth. Soon he will find there are fates worse than being buried alive, for in the abandoned mines and caves beneath Pintalba, there are ravenous teeth in the dark. As a savage predator targets the group with hideous ferocity, Sam and his friends must fight for their lives if they are ever to see the sun again.

Printed in Dunstable, United Kingdom